HAND OF STEEL

Jessi L. Roberts

ISBN: 1733861106
ISBN-13: 978-1733861106

Cover by ERA7
www.deviantart.com/era7
email: era7mechaartist@gmail.com

To my family, who supported me.

There is a glossary of species and planets in the back of the book.

CHAPTER ONE
The Comet's Tail

Sunlight reflected off a bulky space freighter as it flew across the plains toward the spaceport. Scraggly grass whipped in the chilly wind that swept across the cracked dirt below the ship.

I tore my gaze away from the bleak expanse and focused on the ramshackle mining town surrounding the spaceport inn we stayed at. We'd come to Lokostwa for bounties, not a lousy view of flat land with a few distant peaks.

Dad scanned a crowd of miners as they left one of the shafts near the edge of town. All the miners, other than the feathery Torfs, wore tattered clothing that did little to break the wind. Tattoos marked some as slaves. Others were workers whose lives weren't much better.

I shivered and followed Dad. A long-sleeved shirt wasn't enough to keep the chill away. I should've put a jacket in my pack, but to save on weight, I'd only packed my first aid kit and some extra ammunition.

We headed past the slaves without looking for bounties hiding among them. Escaped slaves and criminals hid because they wanted to avoid the mines, or worse, the pits. They wouldn't hide in the very place they wanted to escape.

I brushed dust from my hair. It would have been smart to cut it short before coming to such a dustbowl, but I liked it long. It made me look younger, which gave me the element of surprise.

People tended to dismiss teenage girls without considering them a threat, even if I carried a stun pistol. Lots of girls carried those, but most hadn't spent time in a hunter academy learning to use one.

Dad pulled his datsheet from his pocket and touched an icon. "Rumor has it this Chix is around. Nasty little beast's been kidnapping people and selling them as slaves on the black market, as well as dealing with exotics that get smuggled in." He handed me the datsheet. "With all these workers coming and going, it would be pretty simple to nab a few."

I looked at the datsheet. Unlike the newer models, which were very thin and folded over at least twice, it only folded once.

An image and description of a Chix appeared on the datsheet screen. Nerrini Kazini. No slave tattoo marked her lustrous black fur. She held her bushy tail higher than the top of her head. Golden rings hung from her ears. A few even adorned the flaps of gliding skin that stretched from her ankles to her wrists.

The datsheet read: *Wanted for slave trafficking, kidnapping, association with smugglers, resisting arrest, kidnapping of hunters, murder of two hunters. Bounty: 4,000 Coin*

My shoulders tensed. Maybe the Chix would only reach my waist if I stood next to her, but considering this one killed hunters, we'd have to be careful. I gave the datsheet back to Dad.

Dad brushed dirt out of his red sideburns. "Krys, you okay?" He watched a Torf strut by. The Torf had lost most of his tail feathers, leaving his long tail nearly bare.

I shrugged. "Fine. I just wish we could go after some sort of scammer. This one sounds like she's dangerous."

Dad playfully punched my shoulder. "We can do this. We're Karzils, and she's a Chix."

His words did little to comfort me. Thousands of years of bloody history showed the Chix were perfectly capable of standing toe-to-toe against any military in the galaxy, other than Tupra.

"Come on." Dad headed deeper into Port City, named after the spaceport. Obviously, whoever called it a city had never seen the shining cities of Saddat.

Stone and rusting metal made up most of the buildings. I examined every person we passed, most of which were Torfs with dirt-colored feathers. None stood out as potential bounties, but many of them watched us with suspicion. Even two decades after the war, they still had a rebellious streak. Most likely, they were followers of the radical Free Kin sect that refused to accept the Ordained were put in power by God.

We traveled through the poor outskirts and into the market area of the town where brightly painted stalls stood against smooth stone and steel buildings. A few Gorkam and Torfs tried to sell us trash, or what looked like trash to me. One Gorkam held up a bit of its own shedded exoskeleton. I moved on without pausing. Why would anyone pay for the spotted shell of a giant insect?

A few larger shops and inns stood ahead. Dad stopped and gazed at a tavern in front of us. Unlike the buildings on the outskirts, this stone building had been smoothed and painted with a mural depicting a comet. Below the comet, lettering spelled out *Comet's Tail*.

"From what I know, Nerrini likes to do trade in places like this," Dad said. "Can you go in there and scout it out?"

I clenched my teeth and nodded. Dad's muscular build and the fact that he was a Human on Lokostwa screamed "hunter." He'd attract too much attention.

"Don't engage if you find something." Dad handed me his datsheet. "If Nerrini isn't there, see if anyone else has a bounty on their heads. Don't let them see this."

"I won't." I did my best to shove the apprehension down. *I'm sixteen. I can handle this.*

I pushed open the steel door and stepped into the tavern. The noise of various species talking and shouting assaulted my ears while starchy smells enveloped my nose. From the earthy aroma, I guessed most of the food was plant-based, though a few meat scents clung in the air.

The door clanged shut behind me.

Local Gorkam and Torfs made up at least half the patrons. A few families sat around tables in the center of the room. The edges had rougher customers, most of which kept their backs to the walls. Some even wore their pistols in the open. Another group of the rough bunch stood at the bar or perched on stools.

I hurried to a dark corner near the doorway and sat at a small table. My chair wasn't as close to the wall as I liked, but it would have to do. I scanned the faces again. A bark-colored Chix sat at the bar next to a huge Elba who had various weapons and sharp claws. A pair of Chix and their children sat around one of the tables, their fur dark sable. The mother's coloring was black enough to be Nerrini, but this Chix had a family.

Two more Chix, both with reddish brown fur, sat in a dark alcove. No other Chix were in the tavern.

A young Torf trotted to my table. "What do you want to eat?" His sandy-colored feathers were shiny, hinting that he got paid well enough to care about his appearance.

A menu had been carved into the metal tabletop. I read the first thing on the list. "Fried sarga root."

He scurried away, his claws clicking on the floor.

I leaned back and pulled out Dad's datsheet. I kept it in my lap, hopefully out of sight of any patrons.

The Chix at the bar turned his head. While the right eye was dark purple, the left had been replaced with cybernetics—not a cybernetic eye either. A lens took up most of the eye socket. From the looks of the metal around it, the thing could telescope.

I punched out a description of the camera-eyed Chix on the datsheet. If only I had a modern datsheet, I'd be able to scan his face from a distance. Still, this was better than our really old one.

The info popped up. Only one Chix had an eye like that so I didn't have to scroll through various icons to find the right one.

Chril Korishi: Wanted for slave trafficking, radicalism, terrorism, pirating, murder, illegal medical experiments, experimentation without consent, enslaving of hunters, war crimes, desertion, espionage, and smuggling. 20,000 Coin. Known aliases: Doc. Known associates, Klate, captain of the Deathhorn.

I stared at the number. *Twenty thousand? That's more than we get in a year.*

I touched Klate's name. An image of a dark brown Elba with black stripes and green eyes appeared.

I froze. My gaze moved to the huge Elba next to the Chix doctor. The stripes on his face were identical to the image on the datsheet. Two thick weapons belts crossed his furry chest. A knife and ammunition hung there, along with a pistol at his hip. Considering he'd have been able to gut any Human-sized person with one swipe of his sharp claws, the weapons were overkill.

The young Torf hurried back with a plate of twisted roots. I stuffed the datsheet in my pocket. The Torf dropped the food on my table and scrambled away before I could pay him. Had he seen Klate's image on the datsheet?

He bumped into a Skallan with a cybernetic leg. Scars marred the Skallan's brownish green scales, indicating he'd likely been in the Tupra War. The Torf paused and said something I couldn't hear over the tavern noise before darting into the kitchen.

I picked up a root and bit into it. Under the dirt flavor that most Lokostwan foods carried, it wasn't that bad. I took another bite and forced myself to look at my food. My hands weren't shaking, that was good. I just had to act normal and avoid getting caught staring.

The Skallan with the cybernetic leg looked at me, rose, and headed for the exit. Like many of his species, he stood a few inches taller than most Human men, though I doubted he weighed much more.

I glanced back at the two pirates. Klate swigged some sort of purple juice while the Chix stuffed a large roast bug into his mouth. If I'd only been dealing with one of them, I'd have considered drugging a drink. Trying to take two would likely get Dad and me killed.

I pulled out my datsheet. It still had Klate's profile on it, which included the murder of multiple hunters.

These pirates needed to see justice, but Dad and I couldn't risk it. Maybe we could find some other hunters who were willing to take the risk and give us a cut for the tip-off.

A scaly hand latched onto my shoulder. The cyborg Skallan had somehow snuck up on me.

I grabbed the Skallan's thumb and yanked his hand off my shoulder. Before he could react, I sprang to my feet and bolted for the exit.

The Skallan snatched my wrist. I spun, my shoulder protesting at the yank. With my free hand, I struck at the Skallan's throat.

He swatted my hand away, then twisted my arm behind my back. He grabbed my stun pistol from my belt then wrapped his gangly arm around my neck, not tight enough to cut off my air but enough to tell me he had complete control.

I froze. If only I'd fought back instead of knocking his hand away, I could have escaped.

"Tenned, what are you doing?" Klate strode toward us, his long ears flipped backward in annoyance, though his voice was soft.

My body trembled.

"Looks like a hunter to me." Tenned's meat-scented breath blew in my face. "Get that datsheet off the floor. It will tell you what she is."

Klate bent and scooped the datsheet up.

When had I dropped it?

He touched the screen. "Fifty thousand? Didn't know I was worth that much." He pushed a few more buttons. "Doc, you're worth a good year's wage."

The camera-eyed Chix hopped off the barstool and scurried to stand beside Klate. He didn't even reach the huge Elba's waist. Klate handed him the datsheet.

The other tavern customers circled around. Most of them glared at me, not the pirates. I wouldn't get any help here.

Klate's feline gaze turned on me.

I fought to keep tears from welling up in my eyes. It took all my self-control to hold his gaze.

"Tenned, let her go."

The Skallan, Tenned, released me and stepped back.

Klate stared down at me, his ears now perked forward. "Why are you after my crew, kid?"

I took a few deep breaths in a desperate attempt to control myself. "I—I wasn't after you, just looking for bounties. Not you. We—I only go after less dangerous criminals."

Klate's ears twitched. "Show me your license."

I reached into my pocket and fumbled with my backup license card. Finally, I extracted the tiny card from my pocket and held it up for Klate.

"A point three." He looked over my shoulder at Tenned. "At her rank, she's only targeting petty criminals." He handed it back to me.

Doc held up Dad's datsheet. "Her history says she'd been looking up information on Nerrini Kazini."

Klate grabbed the datsheet and turned it so I could see the picture of Nerrini. "Is this who you were after?"

I nodded.

"You won't have any luck here. That vermin headed to Tupra when her bounty went up."

I relaxed a little. Why was he telling me this?

"You taking this one to Tupra to sell her?" a Torf hissed. "Stinking Loyalist." His feathers stuck upward aggressively.

Sold as a slave on Tupra like a criminal? I wrapped my arms around myself to hide my trembling.

Klate's ear swiveled backward. "I'm not selling a kid, even if she is a Loyalist hunter."

"She can't be alone," Tenned said. "She'll bring her buddies after us if you let her go."

"She wasn't after us." Klate stepped sideways, giving me a clear shot to the door.

I bolted from the tavern into the cold light of Lokostwa's sun.

Dad stood across the street, his back to the wall.

I ran to him. I'd been a disgrace, getting myself in such a mess.

Dad put his hand on his pistol and looked over my shoulder, probably making sure I wasn't pursued.

Klate opened the door and peered through.

Dad pulled his pistol from his belt. He kept it pointed at the ground, an obvious threat.

Klate ducked back into the tavern.

"You can tell me about it after we're away from here." Dad walked fast, deeper into Port City.

As I followed, my body stopped shaking.

When we were far from the Comet's Tail, Dad stopped. "What happened back there?"

I got my breathing under control. "Nerrini wasn't there. I checked some of the others for bounties. That big Elba, he's a pirate captain with fifty thousand on him. They caught me."

Dad went rigid. "Did they hurt you?"

"No. I—I'm fine. Just a little shook up." I looked at the ground. "They took our good datsheet and my pistol." We couldn't replace that stuff until we got a decent bounty. I mentally beat myself. I hadn't been careful enough, then I'd frozen up when they spotted me. What kind of hunter would I make? "I should have been more careful."

Dad hugged me. "It's okay. We can replace the stuff." He released me. "Coming to this planet was a mistake. These locals have no regard for the law. Once we get a decent bounty, we'll go back to Saddat."

"I don't get it. Why'd they let me go?"

Dad shrugged his broad shoulders. "You might've been too much hassle for them. Then again, some pirates have a sense of morals. The Free Kin Bible isn't that different from what we read, just has all the parts about following the law misinterpreted. I don't like hunting them, not when I owe the *Samaritan's* crew."

Even though he'd known Mom and Dad were hunters, the *Samaritan's* captain saved us when I was a baby. Unlike Klate, that captain's list of crimes hadn't included killing hunters. "Shouldn't we report the *Deathhorn's* in the area?"

"Not when they let you go," Dad said. "Come on. We'll try hunting in the market."

I followed after him. Hopefully, the market would be safer, but on a planet full of Free Kin who hated hunters, we'd have to watch our backs.

CHAPTER TWO
Melsha

My stomach growled. After two days, even the dried rations being sold across the street smelled good.

I squeezed the bench I sat on. I hadn't even been able to finish the root at the tavern, thanks to those pirates. Now, we had to save every coin for passage off this stupid planet.

Dad's siblings, Reva and Akar, always had enough to eat. *Maybe we should join with them.* They'd taken in Urkot, who had to be our most inept hunter relative. Surely they'd let us join their team.

Someday, once I gained enough skill to go after pirates and dangerous outlaws, we'd be able to get elite status, then we'd have the coin we needed and free passage between planets.

A Skallan child with a blue thief tattoo on his scaly cheek scurried down the street. By the way his gaze darted around the street, I guessed he was an escaped slave, not one who had served his time and still had a tattoo. I glanced at Dad, who leaned against the corner of a stone building across the street. He hadn't spotted the thief.

My stomach growled again.

The little thief stepped in front of a Gorkam with shopping bags. The thief held out one grubby hand to the huge insect-like creature. "Please, a little coin or food."

The Gorkam's antenna twitched. She reached into one of her bags and pulled out some sort of root.

The thief snatched the root and bit into it. "Thanks!" He darted past me, toward Dad.

I watched him go. I couldn't sentence some kid to years of slavery just because he'd stolen something to ward off starvation.

A Torf, one of the thousands in Port City, strutted down the street, her feathered tail bobbing as she went. She carried a large bag over her back. A red and gold furred himple curled around her neck like a scarf. She kept her shoulders hunched up so the himple hid her cheeks.

That was suspicious. Himples were an exported Tupran species that carried a high price tag and tended to be owned by nobility, not poor Torfs.

I peered closer at the Torf. Though she used the himple to shield her cheeks as best she could, I spotted a yellow slave number tattoo peeking out from under a hasty makeup job. No doubt her other cheek showed her crimes, which were serious enough to get her life as a slave but still leave her some rights.

I peered closer. She had a pistol holstered on her red belt. Other than that, she wore nothing.

My gaze locked with Dad's. He nodded once.

Let the hunt begin.

Dad stepped out of the alleyway and walked ahead of the target. I waited until she'd passed, then followed after her, careful to keep my walk loose and my gaze roving around the street. I touched the stun pistol at my hip, the same model as the one I'd lost in the tavern.

What sort of criminal was she? Obviously a well-traveled one, judging by the himple. Her yellow tattoo meant she hadn't been caught for murder, so she'd be a better target than pirates. Her feathers were well-groomed, not a spiky mess like some Lokostwan Torfs. The scales around her face didn't have the sheen of a young Torf, but they hadn't started to roughen yet.

She darted off the main street, losing Dad, who had stayed ahead of her. I followed her into the side street. Dad followed me, staying far enough back she likely wouldn't notice him, even if she spotted me.

Now, with fewer locals, keeping out of the Torf's sight became harder.

She darted down an even narrower passage between two stone buildings. I jogged to the corner and turned in time to see her look back.

The feathers on her head shot up. She reached for her pistol.

I drew mine and fired.

The Torf fell to the hard earth in a twitching heap of feathers.

I ran to her and pointed the pistol at her. She lay still, other than her breaths, which came fast and ragged.

Dad charged down the alleyway. He patted my shoulder. "Good work." He knelt by the Torf and pulled my dart from her chest. A slight burn mark encircled the feathers around the dart where the electricity had shot into her before the paralysis serum took over.

"Let's see what you're in for." Dad turned the Torf's head and wiped off the makeup, exposing the number tattoo. He pulled our ancient datsheet from his pocket and punched in the number. "Melsha of the Tri-peak Valley Clan. Age thirty-two. Wanted for escaping justice, Free Kin radicalism, and terrorism. Five thousand." Her other cheek bore a slave tattoo, a spear and arrow fashioned into a cross, the symbol of a Free Kin radical.

Dad cuffed her hands behind her back, then did the same with her legs. He wrapped a muzzle around her jaws. With her powerful legs and sharp teeth, we had to be careful.

I holstered my pistol with shaking hands. "She was going to shoot me."

Dad picked up her pistol. "It's a stunner."

Relief pulsed through me. If I'd missed, I wouldn't have died. Still, I'd done well under pressure, much better than the encounter with Klate. Power surged through me. If we kept this up, we'd gain rank and come closer to being elites, though we still had a long ways to go. If Mom were alive, she'd be proud.

The himple chirruped and looked up at me with wide eyes.

"Krys, get the bag, I'll carry Melsha." Dad hefted our prisoner onto his shoulder. If she'd been any bigger, we'd have had to drag her.

I grabbed her bag and slung it over my shoulder where my own pack already hung. What had Melsha been carrying? Rocks?

The himple took a few steps toward me. I slowly reached out to it and ran my hand down its back. It hummed happily and lifted its tail, so I set it on my shoulder. It curled around my neck like a warm scarf.

I hurried after Dad.

The Torf's gaze focused on me. Though her body was paralyzed, she could still move her eyes.

I couldn't meet her gaze, not when I'd condemned her to a life of slavery. No, with her crimes, she'd likely be pitbait. My shot had been meant to capture her, but I might as well have killed her.

We walked through the good part of town, avoiding any places where we could be ambushed. A few Torfs glared at us, but I kept a hand on my pistol, which was enough warning they didn't dare come near us. Finally, we made it to the spaceport.

Guards stood around the edges. Gun turrets towered above them, meant for shooting down any pirates bold enough to attack while slaves loaded mined goods, mostly bendsteel. The valuable flexsteel mined here would only be moved in large space convoys with mercenary guards.

Dad headed for a small boxy freighter that the slaves were leaving. They'd likely finished loading it, so it'd be taking off soon.

A Torf slave stepped in front of Dad, his black hackles raised in a halo around his head. "Put her down, hunter."

I stepped next to Dad and drew my pistol. "Get out of the way."

The Torf glared but backed off. "I hope you die in the dark." The curse hung in the air.

We passed the Torf and made it to the ship. A few slaves darted away. *They're already caught, they shouldn't be so spooked.*

A portly Skallan strode down the ramp. His golden eyes turned toward Dad. "Let me guess, you want passage to Saddat?"

"We'll pay."

The Skallan smiled, exposing yellowed teeth. "A thousand per passenger, unless you're elites."

"I'll give you fifteen hundred. You feed us for the entire voyage," Dad said. "You'll get reimbursed for the prisoner when we get to Saddat. You know how that works."

The Skallan smirked. "Fine, as long as you two hunters work security until we get there. No surrendering if pirates attack, you got that?"

"Deal," Dad said. "By the way, I'm Brok Karzil and this is my daughter, Krys."

"Wurrud," the Skallan said. "What's your rank?"

"I'm a one point five and Krys is a point three." Dad pulled out his license. Even combined, we were nowhere near the rank of five, what we needed to be elites.

Wurrud glanced at the license. "There's a storage room we can dump your scum in." He pointed at the himple wrapped around my neck. "And that thing can stay in a box or the cell. It is not getting loose on my ship."

"I'll lock it up," I said.

Dad walked up the ramp. I followed after him.

A Chix child with dark gray fur swept dust from the top of the ramp. A blue thief tattoo adorned his cheek.

The child's dark blue eyes locked on Melsha.

"Hirami, show them the way to the cell," Wurrud snapped.

"Yes, master." Hirami glared at Dad. "Follow me."

He led us into the belly of the ship and past cells of nigotum fuel, then stacks of bendsteel. The few straps keeping it in place were frayed with age. Dust from various planets covered the floor. *This place is a flying trash heap.*

We stepped through a hatch, then Hirami led us to a small room with a door made of bars and mesh. It was probably used to house animals more often than prisoners. A key hung next to the cell. It held no furnishing, only a hole in the floor for waste, and another in the door for food or water. *We should get her a blanket.*

Dad stepped into the cell and lowered Melsha to the cold floor.

I dumped the bag outside the cell, then pulled the himple off my shoulders and let it loose next to Melsha.

By now, the paralysis serum would be wearing off. I drew my pistol, ready to fire if Melsha tried anything.

Dad unlocked the cuffs on Melsha's legs and hands, then removed the muzzle. He stepped out of the cell and closed the door.

I holstered my pistol.

Melsha shifted herself until she could sit like a broody bird. She ruffled her feathers and then stared at us. "You two have no idea what you've got yourselves into. I suggest you release me now."

A shiver shot down my spine. She spoke as if she was warning us. *It's got to be a bluff.*

"I'll take your threat seriously if I have reason to," Dad said.

The himple sprang onto Melsha's shoulder and curled around her neck. She stroked it with one of her clawed hands. Her gaze focused on me. "If you do take me to the sales ring, keep Flame."

She wanted me to keep her himple? Well, it was kind of cute with its big dark eyes. "I can do that."

Melsha's feathers relaxed. "Thank you."

"We'll get you a blanket and some food." Dad pocketed the keys. "Come on, Krys."

I glanced around. Hirami had vanished. I picked up Melsha's bag and headed through the ship's corridors with Dad behind me. There weren't many rooms. After all, this was a freighter, not a ship meant to have a large crew.

Wurrud stepped in front of us. "I'll show you to the sleeping quarters."

He led us to the front of the ship, where the sleeping alcoves were. Four mattresses lay in the back of human-sized alcoves with sliding doors. Each had a small drawer under it for supplies. Judging by the dust on three of the mattresses, they weren't used often. In the fourth, Hirami lay curled into a ball with his tail wrapped around his body.

"We'll be taking off in an hour." Wurrud stepped through the door hatch and left us in the dusty room.

"Let's see what we've got." Dad opened Melsha's bag and began pulling contents out.

Most of the contents were non-perishable rations, such as sarga roots and a bit of dried meat. None of it looked particularly appetizing. Lokostwa didn't grow good food.

In a front pocket, Dad pulled out the good stuff. Two hundred fifty in flexsteel coin lay in rolls of ten. A civilian datsheet lay next to the coin.

Dad thumbed through the datsheet. "She kept this thing pretty clear. Nothing here we can use, but I'll get this refurbished."

"She must have been planning on leaving the planet." I stared at the roots. If she'd left a bit earlier, she wouldn't have been traveling to her death.

"You okay, Krys?" Dad asked.

I poked at one of the roots. "It's just that I know where she'll end up."

Dad nodded, his green eyes downcast. "From her tattoo and crimes, I'm guessing she's an escaped slave who went terrorist. She needs to be put away."

I kept my focus on the roots. "She won't last long in the pits."

"Maybe she won't go there, but that's not up to us. We just get dangerous criminals off the street. It's okay to leave thieves loose but not terrorists."

I nodded. Still, she didn't have any bullets. That bothered me. If she'd had bullets in the pistol, it would have made it easier for me to think of her as evil. Sure, some people did use bullets for self-defense, but it was kind of silly when a dead body only brought in a quarter of the bounty.

Dad pulled a blanket out of one of the three alcoves. He shook some of the dust off it. "You can take this down to Melsha. Give her some of the roots and water."

Hirami peered from his alcove. Tear stains darkened the fur around his eyes.

I grabbed a bit of the dried meat. "Want some?" By the length of the strips, I guessed the meat came from some sort of snake.

Hirami crawled out of his alcove and snatched the meat from my hand. "The hunter who caught me never fed me." He darted back to his alcove and devoured the dried meat.

"If you're hungry, ask us. We'll give you something to eat," Dad said.

Hirami's tail twitched. "Yer not so bad, fer hunters." Judging by the way his fur curled in on itself, I guessed he'd been underfed.

I'd keep an eye on him over the next week. If he was being abused, maybe we could report that to the Ministry. They were supposed to oversee the slaves and make sure none with blue or yellow tattoos were abused. I doubted they'd care enough to investigate this, but it was all I could do.

I grabbed a handful of roots and headed for Melsha's cell.

Melsha stood with her head held high.

I slid the blanket and roots through the hatch in the bottom of the cell door. "I'll get you some water too."

Melsha grabbed the blanket and roots. Unlike some of the other bounties we'd taken in the past, she met my gaze and held it, but not with the malice I'd seen from so many prisoners. "What made you come after me?" she asked.

"We needed a bounty," I said. "We weren't after anything specific." *And you're a terrorist who needs to be locked up.*

"If you survive, find a different job." Melsha bit into one of the roots and turned away.

CHAPTER THREE
Fire

As I fell, I thrashed in the darkness. I slammed face-first into something and bounced back to the mattress of the alcove. The last remnants of the falling dream submerged themselves in my mind. I tried to roll over and bounced again. *No gravity.*

I listened. The engine still ran so at least we weren't dead in space.

Careful not to send myself bouncing around again, I slid open the hatch to my alcove.

Dull red light illuminated the quarters. Dad opened his alcove. "Krys, get your pistol."

I reached for the drawer under my alcove where my pistol lay.

Hirami ricocheted off the walls of the room and shot to the hatch. He hit the lever beside the hatch. It slid open, and Hirami soared through it and out of sight.

I grabbed my gun belt and buckled it. In zero-g, even that action sent me rolling, but I kept my orientation. My training at the hunter academy saved me from flailing around like an animal, something that had been the subject of many practical jokes.

Dad grabbed our weapons bag and flew from his alcove, pistol in hand. He bounced off the walls, going hand over hand toward the hatch. I headed after him, but I kept my feet positioned downward. Dad flew down the hall like the air had turned to water. Without worrying about keeping his feet pointed down, he outpaced me.

I began to move head first down the corridor to the cockpit. A memory of falling flat on my belly in training after a prankster turned the gravity on entered my mind. I shifted back so my feet pointed down.

The gravity slammed on. I fell to the floor and landed on my hands and knees. I sprang back to my feet and ran after Dad.

I slid around a corner in time to see Dad stumbling to his feet. He coughed.

"I thought the academy gave you zero-g training," I said.

"No time for talking." Dad took off.

Wurrud stepped through the cockpit hatch. "Get ready for a fight."

Dad and I ran into the cockpit, which barely fit the three of us. "Pirates?" Dad asked.

Wurrud's scales had gone pale green. "The *Deathhorn*. They hit us with a hijacker. They're docking now. I sent out a distress call, but it will be too late."

I peered through the cockpit window. Distant stars twinkled. We were in the middle of nowhere. The ship wasn't moving, so the reverse thrusters had worked, but they'd pushed the engine to the breaking point to slow us to safe speeds, something not uncommon when a ship had to stop too quickly. That allowed the hijacker drone to attach to the ship and take over the computers, leaving us helpless, not that the unarmed freighter would be any match for a warship like the *Deathhorn*.

The short-range communication system buzzed.

Wurrud touched the control screen. An image of Klate took up the window. He glared at us, his ears flat against his head and his teeth showing. I took a step back. He was frightening enough in a good mood. Now, he looked like he wanted to gut us.

"He can't see us," Wurrud whispered, his own eyes wide with terror.

"Surrender now and I will spare your lives," Klate growled. "Any attempt at resistance will be crushed."

Wurrud pushed a button so he could talk back. "Stay off the ship or we'll take you in for dead price, pirate. I've hired mercenaries."

Klate growled, deep and menacing. "So be it." His image vanished.

"There's a weapons locker to the left of the hatch," Wurrud said.

Dad stood frozen, his face pale.

"You're not thinking about surrendering, are you, hunter? We made a deal," Wurrud snapped.

Maybe surrender was a good idea. Three of us couldn't take on a whole crew of pirates, could we?

Dad shook himself. "I'm not letting pirates get their hands on my daughter. If they don't kill us outright, they'll sell us on Tupra." He ran out the hatch and opened the weapons locker.

I ran to his side.

Fire grenades and rifles with armor piercing bullets filled the locker.

Dad slung one of the rifles over his shoulder. He clipped five fire grenades to the back of his belt. He already had a half-dozen stunner grenades on the front. He pulled another fire grenade from the stash and held it out to me.

I stared at it. "We don't kill people."

"If those pirates know we're willing to kill, they might back off. Pirates don't attack things that aren't profitable." He pulled a magazine of stunner darts from his bag and handed it to me. "I want you to get to the sleeping quarters and wait there. We'll try to hold them off." He tossed me a mask, meant to stop the stunner grenade's paralysis gasses from knocking us down.

I clipped the magazine to my belt and put on the mask. "I can fight." I'd hit Melsha easily. I could fight pirates.

Dad shook his head. "No, Krys. I'd be trying to protect you instead of fighting. I'll do better if I know you're behind me." He grabbed me in a hug. "I love you."

"Me too." I released him and stepped away.

"Remember, these guys are going to try to kill you. Don't show mercy or surrender. There's no telling what they do to prisoners."

A shudder passed through the ship. The pirates had docked.

"Go, now!" Dad shouted.

I ran to the dormitories and hit the panel by the hatch. It slammed shut.

I waited in the red glow of the emergency lighting. *God, please help us.*

Shots and screams echoed through the ship. I drew my pistol and pointed it at the door. The Torf slave's words came back to me. *"I hope you die in the dark."*

Why did the pirates have to attack us? Dozens of ships flew from Lokostwa to Saddat. The one we'd picked wasn't anything special.

The fighting drew closer. No way Dad could beat the whole pirate crew.

The hatch whooshed open. Dad sprang through, a fire grenade in his hand. Even with the mask covering his face, I saw panic in his eyes.

Where was Wurrud? Had the pirates already got him?

Dad threw the grenade through the hatch. A second later, his eyes widened. He leaped at me, crushing me against the floor.

The grenade bounced back into the room.

A wave of liquid fire washed over us. Pain tore through every nerve of my body.

Pain and a few blurred specters hovering over me were my only companions in the darkness that seemed to go on for ages.

Finally, the darkness and pain released me. My body ached, but it wasn't the debilitating pain that had been my companion in the darkness.

I tried to open my eyes. My left refused to respond, but my right one opened, giving me a view of green. I blinked, but my vision was still blurry, and my thoughts were fuzzy.

A large ship's vibrations thrummed through my bed. Where was I? I had to struggle to keep my eye opened. My traitorous body wanted to sleep, not awaken. Next to me, a machine beeped softly.

My vision cleared enough to let me see a curved ceiling painted in a forest canopy mural. It took all my concentration to turn my head until I could see one of the walls and surrounding beds. So it was an infirmary with walls painted in tree murals? Huge potted plants grew up the walls while other hanging vines draped along the upper wall. A few vines were even climbing along the ceiling and over the light fixtures.

I tried to sit up. My right arm only pushed a little before giving up, and my left side refused to move at all. What was wrong with me? Fear tingled at the edge of my mind, but exhaustion kept it from turning into panic.

A Chix darted across the floor, which was the only thing not painted green. He sprang onto the edge of my bed. His cybernetic eye telescoped toward me then retracted.

It was Klate's crazy doctor.

"How are you feeling?" He waved his hand over my face.

I opened my mouth to speak, but my jaw muscles didn't work right. A raspy croak emanated from my throat.

"Easy," he said. "You've been out for almost five weeks." His tail twitched. "Call me Doc. That's what everyone calls me."

"Get way," I croaked. What had he done to me? I tried to rise but sank back to the bed.

Doc hopped over me, to the other side of the bed, and out of my line of sight. Was I blind on my left side?

Doc's hand touched the skin around my left eye, prompting a strange tingle. What was wrong with me?

An odd sensation moved in my eye socket. Was he yanking my eye out? I tried to move, but he pressed a furry paw to my forehead. I needed to fight, but I was too weak to even resist the touch of a Chix.

Doc released me.

I turned my head enough to see him holding up some sort of black orb. He fiddled with it then reached toward me.

I summoned up all my strength and swung my right hand at his face.

Doc sprang backward off the bed, avoiding the hit. I tried to rise again. This time, I managed to roll onto my left side. A few tubes connected to my right arm tangled around me.

The arm that lay beside my left side was not flesh and blood but steel. I collapsed onto the bed. I'd been made into a cyborg, one that didn't even work. I should have felt anger, but my thoughts were too fuzzy.

Doc sprang onto the left side of the bed and grabbed my head again. Something pressed into my eye socket. Vision shot through my eye. The colors were brighter than they should have been. I tried to blink. Nothing happened.

"It's a state-of-the-art cybernetic eye," Doc said. "I've got a few special features like color enhancement and night vision." He prattled on, using terms I didn't understand and didn't care about.

I tried to push through the fuzzy feeling in my head, to get my mind to work right, but I couldn't fight whatever drugs the crazy doctor had pumped into me.

Next to me, machines beeped faster. Doc glanced at it, his ears perking. "You're getting too excited." He pushed a few buttons on the machine.

Drowsiness flowed through me. "No," I growled. My real eye slid shut.

CHAPTER FOUR
Prisoner

"She should wake up fully this time. I took all the tubes out and tweaked her chip a little."

My eyes snapped open. That is, the real eye opened and the other turned on. Klate sat next to the bed. Doc perched on a nearby table.

I tried to sit up, but my left side moved sluggishly. I sank back to the bed.

Klate touched a button on the side of the bed. The bed bent into a sitting position.

A bit of relief tingled through me. Sitting up made me feel a tiny bit less helpless.

"I'm sorry," Klate said. "I didn't realize it was a fire grenade until it blew." His ears drooped. "Doc did what he could, but we couldn't—" He motioned to Doc with his thumb. "Better get the mirror."

Doc sprang off the table and ran across the room. He came back with a mirror, which he unrolled in front of me.

A half-cybernetic freak stared at me from the mirror. I touched my head and the thing in the mirror touched hers too. My hair was little more than fuzz and only covered the right side of my head. Fake gray skin and metal had replaced my left side. There had been no attempt at making the cybernetics look human.

"You monsters." My voice came out as a thin rasp.

Klate flinched.

Doc rolled up the mirror and ran across the floor to the cabinet. He grabbed a bottle of water then raced across the room and sprang onto my bed.

I swung my real fist at his face, aiming for his cybernetic eye. He did a backflip onto the table.

If I'd been in good shape, my fist would have connected.

"You need to drink. I took out your feeding tube." Doc's tail twitched. "I also unhooked the anti-atrophy machines."

Where was Dad? Had they captured him too? I looked past Klate. No other beds in the infirmary were occupied. Had he escaped? My mind flashed back to the blast. He had thrown himself over me. No way he'd survived that.

"You killed him!" I launched myself at Klate. This time, my cybernetic arm moved, just enough that I made it out of the bed. My cybernetic leg snagged on the edge of the bed.

Klate caught me.

I slammed my real fist into his nose. He grunted and shoved me back into the bed.

I tried to rise again. Klate placed one huge clawed hand on my shoulder. His ears swiveled backward in annoyance.

Dad's words came back to me. *Keep your emotions down until you're safe.* I'd have to mourn later.

Klate glanced away. "We never had a chance to save him."

"Don't talk about him," I choked out.

Klate took his hand off my shoulder and backed away.

Doc's tail twitched. "Can you move your cybernetics?"

I clenched my cybernetic fist. The more I concentrated, the more I felt the cybernetics. I tried to move my foot. It twitched a little but didn't move much.

"Keep working at it," Doc said. "The chip in your head will learn from your movements. It interfaces better the more you move."

A chip in my head? Doc had a bounty for illegal experimentation. I shuddered. He now had a perfect captive for whatever experiments he wanted. No one would come to save me.

"Leave me alone." The cautious part of me told me to play along and be nice, but what did I have left to lose? I'd become a prisoner in my own body.

Klate backed away. "I'll go. Let Doc help you. The sooner you're better, the sooner you can get off this ship." He ducked through a hatch and out of the room.

Doc watched me, his tail twitching.

I glared at him.

Doc hopped onto my bed and set the water down in a cup holder next to my right hand. "You can drink when you want. I'll bring you some food later." He jumped back onto the table, then onto the floor. He ran to the other side of the room and climbed up a hanging plant next to some cabinets. Once he'd made it into the huge pot, he lay down and curled his tail around himself.

What did the pirates want to do with me? With ugly cybernetics, they couldn't sell me to a brothel. Tupran pit fights? Cyborgs were popular in pit fights. It made no sense to spend money on cybernetics for an enemy and let them walk away. Why couldn't they have killed me? Whatever they wanted with me, it had to be bad.

I moved my real arm and leg. Though weak, they worked okay. They just needed exercise. The minor burn scars on my skin would heal in time.

I focused on my cybernetic side. The metal on my leg glistened in the white light of the infirmary. The cybernetics were obviously not meant to blend in with the rest of my body, unlike the sort the nobility would choose.

I lifted my left hand to get a better look at it. This time, it responded, though it jerked toward my face unnaturally.

With only three strong fingers and a thumb with a tiny bit of replacement skin on the finger tips, this had to be military style, not civilian. Shining steel covered the rest of it, the same as my leg. Both had some sort of extension partway down so I could lengthen my arm and leg. No replacement skin covered the arm and leg, though I did have replacement skin on my foot, which had four toes that stretched back into the cybernetic foot much farther than Human toes.

I touched the steel on my cybernetic arm. A tingle shot through it. There were sensory receptors planted in the steel. I touched my face. Fake skin covered it completely, leaving no steel to be felt. When I pressed harder, I realized that some of the stuff under my skin was probably muscle and bone, not steel. Steel and fake skin replaced my nose. Breathing through it made me feel stuffed up.

My real fingers traced around my fake eye. I ventured to touch it. It had a smooth surface. I saw my fingers through the eye, every wrinkle perfectly clear.

I moved the toes on my cybernetic leg, then worked with my cybernetic arm, forcing it through various movements. Every time I repeated a movement, it was smoother. I had to get to the point I could walk again. Even if I couldn't escape, maybe I could throw myself out the nearest hatch. Then, I'd be with Mom and Dad.

Dad sacrificed himself so you'd live. No. Throwing myself into space wasn't an option, not unless I knew for sure that I'd be tortured.

I kept moving my cybernetic leg. If Doc would leave, I could try walking.

The lights in the infirmary dimmed to mimic nighttime.

I kept working with my cybernetics, forcing them to do what I wanted. I also moved my real limbs, testing them and working out the stiffness. I needed to be ready for planetfall, most likely Tupra. Problem was, hunters weren't welcome there. Even Akar and Reva wouldn't dare hunt on the rogue planet.

My cybernetic eye picked up more light than my real one. I'd have to adjust to that, though it could be useful.

The water sparkled beside my bed. My throat ached for it.

I reached for it but pulled my hand away. The pirates wanted me to drink it.

I imagined the water sliding down my parched throat. If I didn't drink, I'd die, or the crazy doctor would force it into me.

I grabbed the water and drank it in a few greedy gulps. My stomach churned, but the water stayed down.

I adjusted the bed and closed my eye. Images of Dad entered unbidden. I tried to shove them down. They refused to leave. I opened my eye.

Doc slumbered in the plant.

Tears streamed from my eye, but I kept myself from sobbing. I couldn't let a pirate see my weakness.

What did it matter? They'd been messing with me while I'd been unconscious. I shuddered at the thought. Still, my instinct stopped me from crying.

Finally, sleep came.

Claws clicked across the floor. I opened my eye. The lights had brightened, signaling morning, ship time.

Melsha stood a short distance from my bed, a tray of food in her hands and the fuzzy himple coiled around her neck.

I adjusted the bed into a sitting position.

"How are you feeling?" she asked.

"Like I'd rather be dead," I snapped.

Melsha's feathery tail drooped. "Sorry. None of us wanted this to happen."

My eye narrowed. "You're one of the pirates, aren't you?"

Melsha bowed her head. "Yes, though I like to think of us as freedom fighters. Most of what we do is smuggling and freeing slaves."

Maybe Melsha wanted to pretend she was one of the good guys, but without slavery, the criminals would be running loose in the streets.

Melsha set the plate of food on the table.

The food steamed. It consisted of a strange slice of blue bread, a bit of meat, and three circular narna fruits.

My stomach growled.

I glanced around the room. Doc still lay curled in his potted plant.

I grabbed the plate of food and bit into the orange fruit. It had the bland taste of something that had been picked a few weeks ago, but my stomach pleaded for more. I finished the fruit and grabbed the meat with my good hand. I ate that before moving on to the strange bread. It had a sweet but grassy taste. For being space rations, the food tasted pretty good.

Melsha shifted from foot to foot. Her tail swished.

I swallowed the last of the bread. "Why are you doing this?"

"Because you're not bad for a hunter," Melsha said.

"Since when do pirates care about that?" I pushed. If she got mad and killed me, I wouldn't have lost anything.

Melsha's feathers drooped. "We have morals."

"Your captain killed Dad." I clenched both fists.

"I warned you." Melsha's lips curled back, almost exposing her teeth and her hackles shot up. "Klate was trying to protect his crew. He never wanted to kill your father."

I glared at her. "And what happened to the captain of the ship you attacked? Bet you killed him too."

"No. We sold him on Tupra. Klate would have let him go free until he saw the state Hirami was in. Poor kid looks like he's ten, but he's thirteen. That captain only fed him scraps."

So that's what they'll do with me if I can move. Then again, I could probably escape slavery if the chip in my head wasn't rigged to kill me. Anger flared. Doc had done all this without getting my permission, disobeying multiple laws to do it. Were the cybernetics even legal, or were they modified to the point of being illegal for civilian use?

"Klate only sells people into slavery if they deserve it," Melsha said.

"I bet hunters deserve it," I snapped.

Melsha sighed. "He won't sell you. I vouched for you."

And pirates always tell the truth. Perhaps he kept me alive because his twisted view of justice meant he thought I deserved punishment, but not death.

Hirami darted into the room and jumped onto the table so he was eye level with Melsha. "Amellia said she's gonna teach me how t' fly!" He spread his arms, which stretched the thin membrane that passed between them and his legs. "She says I'll be a super good pilot 'cause I'ma Chix and we have fast reflexes."

Doc climbed out of his potted plant.

"Why didn't ya fly the *Deathhorn*?" Hirami cocked his head at Doc. "Youra Chix."

"I don't like flying," Doc said. "I can help Ralkom fix the intricate parts. Flying's too wild."

I watched the pair chatter away, their tails twitching. The little slave was thrilled to be a pirate, and the others treated him like an equal.

After chattering with Doc, Hirami bolted from the room.

Doc pulled a round ball about the size of his fist from the cabinet near his plant.

He tossed it in my direction. Without thinking, I caught it in my right hand.

"Now toss it to your left," Doc ordered.

My eye narrowed. I wasn't going to be ordered around, not by a mad scientist.

Melsha glanced at Doc, then to me. "How about I help you stand instead?"

I laid the ball on my bed. I swung my real leg over the edge of the bed, then swung the cybernetic one over. I still had a fair amount of my thigh but past that, the leg was cybernetic. Like my arm, the crazy doctor hadn't even attempted to make it look like a real leg.

Melsha grabbed my cybernetic arm.

I stiffened at the pirate's touch. *Better her than one of the others.* My feet touched the floor. I put weight on my legs. My real knee trembled, weak from the lack of exercise. The cybernetic one stood firm though my balance was off.

Melsha pushed her feathery shoulder under my cybernetic arm.

I moved my artificial leg into a less shaky position so I could put more weight on it. My real leg trembled but held.

Melsha stepped away. I grabbed the bed with my real hand. My legs supported me.

A wave of dizziness washed over me. I swayed, and the cybernetics didn't compensate. I fell.

Melsha scrambled to grab me but missed.

I face planted into the floor, my real arm not strong enough and my cybernetic too slow to catch me. I lay there for a second, catching my breath. I hadn't been hurt, at least not badly.

Melsha squatted down to help.

I ignored her hand. I got my hands under my body and pushed myself into a crawling position, then tried to rise. By using the bed as support, I made it to my feet. My arm trembled, too weak to hold my weight.

Without asking, Melsha helped me back onto the bed.

The ball fell from the bed. Melsha scooped it up and handed it to me. "Keep practicing. If you can use your arm, that will help with your balance."

Doc watched, unmoving for the first time since I'd met him.

Melsha picked up my empty plate. "Got to cook for the rest of the crew." She headed through the exit hatch.

"There's a button on the side of your bed. Press it if you need something." Doc scurried after Melsha.

I tossed the ball in the air and caught it with my real hand, then tossed it to my left hand. My cybernetics closed on the ball and held it. I kept juggling the ball.

My cybernetic fingers closed too early. The ball bounced off my fingers and rolled across the floor, coming to a stop next to one of the many plants. Maybe I shouldn't be practicing. Then, Klate couldn't sell me. They'd have to throw me into space or something.

Claws clicked softly outside the hatch. Klate peered into the room.

I did my best to glare at him, but with only half my face working, I doubted I got the message across.

Klate padded into the room. He stooped to pick up the ball then laid it on my bed. "If you ever want to talk, let me know."

"Get out of here," I snapped.

Klate backed toward the hatch. "I hope you can forgive me." He ducked through the hatch.

My stomach clenched. God said to forgive, but this? He'd wrecked everything. I went back to tossing the ball from hand to hand. If I had to, I could pretend I had more trouble with my cybernetics than I did. Then I'd catch them by surprise.

I squeezed the ball in my cybernetic hand. The ball's shape began to flatten. I let up on the pressure then grabbed the ball in my real hand and squeezed. No matter how hard I tried, I couldn't squish the ball with my real hand.

My cybernetic hand was stronger than my real hand, perhaps stronger than a normal Human hand. Something that strong could be a weapon.

CHAPTER FIVE
Crew

With Melsha's help, I learned to walk in a week.

"You're doing well," Melsha said as I stumbled across the floor.

My cybernetic leg still felt heavy and unwieldy, but I could run if I had to. I couldn't let anyone know that. I took another step and purposefully slipped.

Melsha caught me and pulled me to my feet. If I had fallen, I'd have been able to catch myself with my cybernetic hand. That thing worked really well.

Doc perched in one of the potted plants near the ceiling. He watched, his tail twitching sporadically.

I walked across the room and back to my bed.

Klate stepped into the room.

I stiffened. What did he want now?

Klate pulled something from his pocket. My datsheet. He crossed the room and stopped in front of me. "I thought you might want this back. I added a Free Kin Bible to it. You only had a Loyalist one." He held the datsheet out.

I hesitated, my instincts telling me not to take anything from the pirate captain.

Klate waited.

I snatched the datsheet and walked away from Klate. I climbed onto my bed and flipped open the datsheet. An image of both my parents and me as a toddler took up the screen. It was the last picture I had of Mom. Now, I'd lost both of them. *I'll carry on your legacy, once I get off this ship.* If I ever escaped, I could go back to hunting. I could make them proud. Maybe I could even bring in Klate.

A presence loomed behind me.

I turned my head.

Klate stood only a few steps away. His ears drooped.

"You looked at this whole thing, didn't you?" I clutched the datsheet to my chest.

Klate lowered his head. "I wanted to know what kind of person you and your dad were."

"And what did you decide?" I demanded.

Klate bowed his head. "I should have done things differently, tried to get a surrender."

I stayed silent, not trusting myself to speak. I couldn't let grief show, not while I was captured.

After standing in silence for a few minutes, Klate spoke again. "Now that you're in better shape, you should sleep in the crew quarters. We don't want you in the way if someone gets hurt."

I glared. I couldn't sleep in a room full of pirates.

Klate's ears twitched. "You'll only have to deal with it for seven weeks. After that, you'll be on Tupra."

I said nothing.

Klate ducked through the open hatch and out of sight.

Seven weeks until they made it to Tupra? Where could we be? Even though the *Deathhorn* was an older ship, it couldn't take more than five weeks to cross Ordained space, six if they were avoiding enemies. They couldn't sell me on Ordained planets, so they needed to go to Tupra to get a good price for me. Then again, they might be headed for Korska. Since my race didn't live anywhere past Korska, I'd be an exotic slave there, bringing a high price if some alien buyer bought me.

"Want to practice walking some more?" Melsha asked.

"I'm done," I snapped. I began thumbing through pictures on my datsheet. Pictures of Dad and me appeared. I sniffed. I'd lost so much.

Melsha watched me for a while then stepped through the hatch. Doc followed.

I wiped tears from my eye. One sad advantage of the cybernetic eye was I didn't have to worry about impaired vision from tears. I thumbed through the photos on the datsheet, examining every last one of them. I let the tears flow, but I kept myself from crying. Once I started, I doubted I'd be able to stop, and then the crew would see me weak.

My stomach growled.

I laid the datsheet on the table. With no one in the room, I could practice running before Melsha brought food.

I stretched my real leg and hurried across the room. The fast walk worked okay, but could I run? I turned back toward my bed and ran. I made it five steps, then my cybernetic leg slipped out from under me and I fell. I caught myself. At least my arm had decent reactions. I could practice it without bringing much attention to myself.

I stood and ran. This time, I made it to the bed. I ran back toward the other wall but fell. My real knee slammed painfully into the hard floor.

I climbed to my feet. My knee ached, but I could always fall again to hide the injury if I had to.

The infirmary's hatch whooshed open. The Skallan who had grabbed me in the tavern strode into the room, his red eyes narrowed. "What are you doing?" he demanded.

I froze, my mouth now dry. My eyes landed on his cybernetic foot, which was nearly identical to mine.

He stormed toward me, only stopping once he was close enough his breath blew on my face. "Klate and Melsha might think you're some sort of pet, but I know what you are, hunter. You step out of line, and I'll make sure you're sold to the worst master I can find."

Claws clicked on the floor.

The Skallan turned toward the sound. I took a few steps away from him.

Melsha stepped through the hatch. A bready scent wafted off her, but she carried no tray of food. "Tenned, what are you doing in here?" Her eyes narrowed.

He shrugged. "Talking to the prisoner." He stepped around Melsha and left the room.

She turned to me. "Thought you could eat in the mess hall today." She shifted from foot to foot, her tail swaying.

My hunger evaporated. Eat with the pirates? Eating around Doc was bad enough, but eating in the same room as Tenned?

Melsha touched my real arm, her clawed hand gentle. "I'll stay next to you if that would help."

A bit of the fear lifted, even though it shouldn't have. Melsha was a pirate like the rest of them and a terrorist as well.

I stood, careful to put enough weight on my injured knee. "I'll go." What choice did I have? Klate probably wouldn't let me eat until I did what he wanted. Anger flared through me. Other than running, I hadn't had any sort of victory. The pirates had forced me to do everything they wanted me to do.

Melsha hopped through the hatch.

I limped to the hatch. So far, I hadn't been out of the infirmary.

I held on to the edge of the hatch as I stepped through. A railing ran along the hallway, something to allow people to move if the gravity went out.

I grabbed the railing.

Melsha turned back. "Follow me."

I followed her through the sleeping quarters and into the mess hall. Most of the pirates already sat or stood around tables.

I counted nineteen crew members, including Klate. Other than Hirami, who I didn't consider crew, Doc was the only Chix, not a surprise since they'd won the Tupra War. Only one other Elba sat at a table. The spears crossed in a red X staining her cheek fur symbolized she'd committed piracy and was given no rights as a slave. There were six Torfs, five Skallan, a trio of common Humans, and a couple hirsut Humans. I tried not to stare at the hairy Humans. They barely looked human with all that hair covering their faces. From what I knew, they came from Korska or somewhere even more distant.

Three long tables occupied the room, but the pirates only stood at one of them. The other two were empty.

Melsha led me to the empty table farthest from the other pirates. "I'll get you something to eat." She headed toward the kitchen, leaving me alone.

I sat at the table with my back to the nearest wall. Tenned watched me, his red eyes narrowed.

I hunched down and tried to make myself smaller. He kept glaring.

What am I doing? I straightened myself and glared back. No pirate was going to make me cower.

Melsha strutted to the table with two plates of food. She set one in front of me and stood with her plate on the table. Like most Torfs, she ate standing up. She took a bite of her bread and then noticed the direction I stared. Her hackles stood.

The old Skallan looked away.

I relaxed but kept my eye on him.

"He's Klate's second in command, a good man but not very friendly. Probably best if you avoid him," Melsha said. "He's had a hard life."

"I'll try." I grabbed a piece of bread. This time, Melsha had mixed some sort of berry into it, giving it a sweet taste.

I glanced at Melsha's crossed spear tattoo. For a Free Kin radical and terrorist, she'd treated me well, and I was her enemy. "How did you get that bounty on your head?" I asked.

Melsha sighed.

My gut clenched. Had I overstepped my bounds? Then again, what if I had?

Melsha finally spoke. "My father died fighting in the Tupra war. My family managed to get by without going hungry, but my friends weren't so lucky. I spoke out against the Company, the people you call the Ordained. Someone reported me for not acknowledging the Company's divine authority. Before I knew what was happening, I was on an auction block with these tattoos." Melsha touched her cheek. "All because I was Free Kin and not Loyalist."

A bit of guilt settled in my stomach. Dad and I had hauled Free Kin to the auction block before. I tried to remind myself Melsha deserved to be a slave, but I couldn't get my feelings to agree with my logic. She'd been so good to me.

"Klate attacked the ship we were on, freed all the slaves." Melsha gazed at Klate. "I went back to Lokostwa where my family was. Never stayed with them for long. I couldn't risk it. I walked by the slave auction block at least once a week." She smiled. "I blew up the whole block and the slave cages around it. Freed them all." She ruffled her feathers. "I hadn't thought to wear something to hide my identity. With the higher bounty, I had hunters after me. I almost got caught, then I saw Klate. I pleaded to join his crew. He took me on as a cook."

We finished eating in silence, then Melsha stood. "I'll take you to the sleeping quarters and get you settled in before the rest of the crew gets there."

She led me to the crew quarters.

Both walls had alcoves with doors that made up the private beds for each crew member, much like Wurrud's ship, though these were clean.

Only one person lay in an alcove, a hirsut Human. Dark brown hair streaked with gray covered his entire face, leaving his features hidden.

Melsha opened the sliding door on an alcove. "You can stay in this one. I sleep in the one across from you, so if you need anything, you can ask me."

I glanced at Melsha's sleeping spot. There used to be a second above the first, but the top one's mattress had been knocked out so Melsha would have more room.

I climbed into my new quarters. It had plenty of room because it was made with Skallan in mind. "Thanks."

"You're welcome."

I shut the sliding door. Light shone through the thin white surface. A small drawer was set into in the alcove's wall. I opened it. My pack lay inside. It smelled of smoke and had a few new burn marks, but it was my pack, the one I'd had before we'd been attacked. I dug through it, finding my handcuffs and some rope, my change of clothes, as well as other supplies, but no weapons. I stuffed it back in the drawer.

I passed the day in my alcove and read my Bible, then cross referenced it with the Free Kin one. The Free Kin one was almost word-for-word the same as my own Bible until I came to

Romans 13, where a few words were changed around, emphasizing that authorities punished evil. I glanced back at my own version, the Loyalist version. *Let everyone be subject to their rulers, for there are no rulers but those ordained by God. Whoever resists their rulers resists God's ordained, and they will receive damnation. Rulers are not a threat to the loyal, but to the disloyal. Do you want to be free from fear of the Ordained? Then remain loyal and you will be praised. For the ministers are God's servants, but if you do wrong, be afraid, for the ministers do not bear the sword in vain; for they are the ministers of God, revengers to execute wrath upon them that do wrong.*

Klate had left a note beside this entry. My finger hovered over the note. Part of me didn't want to open it, but then again, he'd never find out. Dad had always said I should know how my enemy thought. I opened the note. *Note in the Free Kin version, the authorities ordained by God reward good and punish evil. The Company punishes good and rewards evil. Because of that, they cannot be God's ordained. The wording in the Loyalist version has changed most of the mention of good and evil to loyal and disloyal in an attempt to remove morality from the verses, thereby forcing people to follow evil rulers.*

So this explained Klate's actions. He held no one in authority over himself, which meant no one had more right to judge who lived and died or who was enslaved than he did. Maybe he even considered himself ordained.

I found the bounty list on the datsheet and looked him up again, noting the multiple murders, war crimes, and slave dealing, among other things. The info on Klate's past was sketchy, but it seemed he'd been born on Saddat, then switched sides during the war. It was rumored he had a wife and daughter on Tupra, but there wasn't any info about them. Had he saved me because I reminded him of his daughter?

Outside the alcove, feet, some clawed and others booted, tramped across the floor as the pirates got ready for bed. I put the datsheet into the drawer and lay on my side. With a bit of concentration, my cybernetic eye switched off.

I lay there for over an hour while the pirates went to sleep. Snores penetrated the thin door, their sounds grating. I could never sleep, not surrounded by enemies. I eased open the door and stepped to the cool floor.

I crept toward the exit hatch. My cybernetic foot, though covered in fake skin, made more noise than I liked. Almost all the doors to the alcoves were closed. Judging by the size of the alcove near the door, I guessed an Elba slept there.

I made it through the hatch and into the hallway. So far, so good. From the ship's vibrations and slight rumble, I guessed we were behind the primary engines. I turned left and headed away from the vibrations. The holds were generally as far away from the engines as possible. I opened a few more hatches and closed them behind me. From what I'd gathered, the hallway was along the edge of the ship, making it easy for the crew to get to the hold without going through the infirmary. The other rooms had no hallway, just a clear path to the next hatch.

By the time I made it to the hold, my real leg ached from the exertion. I needed to exercise more. The ramp into the hold, which had a ceiling twice as high as any other room, was a bit hard for me to walk down, but I made it.

Only a few dim lights shone in the hold. My real eye couldn't adjust to the dimness of the room, but my cybernetic eye took in everything. Cells of nigotum stood strapped to one wall near the ramp. Why did the pirates have nigotum? Their ship used perital for fuel. Since nigotum came from Tupra, Saddat, and Chibbink, it wasn't very good for trading because it was a similar price on all the planets but Lokostwa.

I thought back to Wurrud's ship. It had a little more nigotum than this. So that was where they got it.

Empty cages for slaves stood along another wall. I shuddered a little. If I didn't behave, I'd likely end up in one of those cages.

A stack of strange fluffy bales sat in the corner of the hold. There weren't many of them. When I got closer, I saw they were made of blue leaves. They smelled like Melsha's bread. I'd never seen the plant before. Was it from Tupra?

I crawled onto the stack and wedged myself between two of the soft bales. I shivered. I'd forgotten to bring a blanket. The hold, being far from the engines, had a chill to it. I pressed my Human side against the bale and closed my eye. My cybernetic eye blinked off.

I fell into a fitful sleep.

A blanket settled over me. I pulled it tight, grateful for the warmth. Where had it come from? My eye opened and my cybernetic one switched on in time to see Klate's tail vanish through the hatch above. How something his size managed to sneak around was beyond me. Dad's words came back to me. *Never underestimate an Elba's stealth. Their hearing is sharper than any other intelligent species so they learn to walk without making a sound.*

I nestled under the blanket. For once, I allowed myself to enjoy something Klate had given me. I couldn't sleep here without some sort of warmth.

CHAPTER SIX
Storm

I jogged through the corridor to the cockpit. It rarely received the crew's traffic, leaving it clear for me to exercise. I made it near the cockpit, turned around and jogged past the captain's quarters and back toward the crew's quarters. If we were landing soon, I needed to be in shape, even if I didn't recognize the name the pirates called the planet. Though Klate acted like he wouldn't sell me, I had to be ready to escape if he'd been tricking me.

Voices emanated from the captain's quarters. I took a few steps backward and put my ear to the hatch.

"The sooner we pawn her off, the better." From the slight rasp of the voice, I guessed it was Tenned. "We spent way too much coin on her the way it is."

"I'm not leaving her on Derbis," Klate growled. "They wouldn't take her anyway."

"Fine. Someone on Tupra might take her. Watch she doesn't sabotage the *Deathhorn* before we make it back there. She should be locked up, not free to roam and find a way to get revenge."

Anger surged through me. They were going to pawn me off. I clenched both fists and imagined my steel one slamming into Tenned's chin.

Booted footsteps headed toward me. I scrambled away from the hatch.

It whooshed open. Tenned stepped through.

"What are you doing here?" he snapped.

I stood tall. "Exercising."

Tenned glared.

Klate ducked through the hatch. "Krys, we're about to land on Derbis. Would you like to see the landing?"

I glanced at Tenned. In this case, Klate had to be the safer option of the two. "I guess."

"Follow me."

I followed Klate past Tenned and to the cockpit. Three seats were bolted to the floor. A hirsut woman sat in one chair. The hair covering her face and head had turned gray with age, but her dark eyes were still sharp.

Klate waved his hand at her. "This is Amellia. She's our pilot."

Amellia smiled. "Nice to meet you."

I nodded.

"Well, strap in." Amellia pushed a button. "We're coming up on Derbis. Brace yourselves."

Wasn't artificial gravity supposed to make landings smooth? I sat in a chair and buckled the harness attached to the seat.

Klate did the same.

The *Deathhorn* turned. Below us, a planet floated in the blackness of space. When I'd first heard the name, I assumed the pirates were using some other name for one of the Ordained planets. I'd been wrong. None of the three Ordained planets had continents like this. This wasn't Tupra or Korska either.

The *Deathhorn* dropped toward the planet. As we approached, I spotted two continents, one near the equator and another farther north, or south depending on how we were coming at the planet. We shot over the equator continent and headed toward the one near the pole. A gigantic dark bay lay at the edge of steely gray mountains. We soared over a storm system higher than the mountains themselves.

Shudders wracked the ship as it entered the atmosphere.

I clutched the edge of my seat and glanced at Klate. He showed no fear. Hopefully, this was normal.

From what I could tell, the mountains were made of some sort of natural metal or steel that shone in the light.

Amellia twisted the old ship through mountain valleys. "Hold on!" she shouted.

Ahead of us, a landing strip ran along the side of the mountain. Judging by its placement, someone had to cut the side of the mountain to make a flat spot for landing.

The *Deathhorn* fell like a wingless bird, slammed into the runway, and bounced.

Amellia flipped a few switches. The ship slid to a stop, throwing me against my seat belt.

Amellia drove the ship off the runway and into a shallow cave.

Klate unbuckled himself and stood. "Good landing."

I tried to relax. If that was a good landing, I didn't want to see a bad one.

Amellia began powering down the ship. "Sorry, it was a bit rough. That landing strip's not long enough."

I unbuckled myself and stood. My real leg trembled a little.

Klate strode past the captain's quarters and through the mess hall. I stepped through the hatch and went after him, careful to stay far enough back it didn't look like I was following him.

Soon, the entire crew fell in behind him. Klate made it to the hold and opened the hatch, which dropped down to make a ramp.

Klate turned to us. "Remember, most of these people don't speak Spacer, and they're not used to foreigners. Common Humans can get by easier than the rest of us. Also, stay close to the ship. If you hear sirens, get inside. The storms here are bad."

The rest of the crew yawned or sniffed the fresh air. They'd had this briefing before, so it was probably more for my benefit.

Klate stepped on the ramp and walked into the cavern. The crew streamed out after him. Most of them carried their pistols. Only Klate carried his rifle. He led us out of the cave and into the sunlight.

My feet touched the soft grass. I took in a deep breath of non-filtered air.

A metallic scent combined with swamp smell entered my cybernetic nose. Had Doc messed up when he changed my nose? This wasn't a normal planet smell, especially since we were far from swamps.

I bent down and plucked a handful of grass and black dirt from the ground. I sniffed it. It smelled of grass, but the swamp scent still clung to it. So it wasn't my nose, but the planet.

Huge metal mountains towered over us. The only green places were the ledges, some of which appeared natural, while others, like the one we'd landed on, were too big and flat to be natural. Along the edge of the mountain, windows and doors were carved into the cliff wall. A few Humans stepped through the doors and came toward us while others peered through the thick windows.

About a dozen Humans, most with dark hair and tanned skin, watched us. The women had no facial hair. A few men had beards. Were these Earth Humans? Their dark complexion and delicate features meant they weren't common Humans, and the lack of hair showed they were far from hirsut.

Melsha stepped next to me. Did she plan to guard me for my time here, or had the pirates decided I wasn't going to escape?

Hirami bolted up a tree with purple leaves. The tree, though large, bent under his weight.

A man with black hair and dark eyes stepped from the others. "Greetings, Klate." He spoke with a thick accent.

Klate bowed his head slightly. "Greetings, Fer."

Fer looked past Klate. "What do you have to trade?"

"We've got a good haul of nigotum," Klate said. "We'll trade it for some perital, leaf bales, milk, and turkeys."

Klate and Fer began haggling over the trade value of their supplies. Turkeys came up multiple times.

I gazed at the ledge of the mountain, looking for anything that could be turkeys or produce milk.

A gray, four-legged creature with horns grazed on a higher ledge above us. It looked like something that could be milked, possibly a smaller relative to the targans of Chibbink. A flock of gray birds leaped off an even higher cliff and flapped over us, their bodies almost too big to stay aloft. They turned and landed on another ledge. A gray and white animal with a fluffy tail ran after the birds and barked at them. From the shape of its body, I guessed it was a predator, likely some relation to a kark but not as big or dangerous.

"Turkeys are the birds," Melsha said. "The hoofed ones are goats and the thing chasing the turkeys is a dog."

A boy climbed down the cliff and toward the big ledge where the *Deathhorn* sat. The turkeys ran out of sight with the dog hot on their tails.

I walked away from Melsha and to the edge of the ledge we'd landed on. A valley opened below. Multiple ledges with trees and grass huddled against the side of the mountain. A few trails were carved between the ledges where goats grazed. A Human rode a gigantic bird behind a large herd of goats.

"You can look around, but stay close to the ship," Melsha warned. "The storms here can be bad, and there are only a handful of locals who speak Spacer."

I nodded. This wasn't going to be an easy planet to escape, not with the locals being friendly to Klate and the rough terrain. I prayed the bird the Human rode wasn't a native to this planet. With the curved beak, it had to be a predator, a predator that could take my head off with one peck.

I headed back toward the ship, but one of the trees distracted me. I approached it and plucked a purple leaf off a branch. I sniffed it. It smelled like Melsha's bread. I bit into it. Sure enough, it tasted much like the bread. At least when I ran, I knew one plant I could eat.

I walked up the ramp and into the *Deathhorn*. The pirates were moving the nigotum cells off the ship. I walked past them and crawled into the bed that I'd made from leaf bales.

I couldn't sleep, not with the pirates awake and my plans pulsing through my head. I listened to their chatter as they hauled out the nigotum and some of the other supplies.

At last, the pirates retired for the night. Without the rumble of the engines, the silence set me on edge. Sneaking around with nothing to muffle my sounds could be risky.

I stood and examined the hold. The hatch stood open, probably to get some airflow in the ship now that the fans were off. Were the people here so peaceful the pirates didn't fear a boarding party?

I took stock of what I needed. A bag for sure. I'd have to carry quite a few supplies. A weapon would be a good idea too. Most of the locals hadn't appeared heavily armed, but there could be predators around.

I crept from the ship. Overhead, a blue star and a silver moon cast their light on the metallic mountains, which sparkled in the darkness.

If there were indeed predators around, the Humans would have guns, and they'd probably be easier to steal than pirate weapons. I stalked to the nearest door embedded in the mountainside and examined the ball-like handle. Why didn't these Humans have normal door handles? I tried to turn the strange knob both ways. It wouldn't move. So these people locked up at night. With pirates on the loose, that was a good idea.

I moved on to the next door set in the cliff side. The knob turned under my grip. I eased the door open and stepped into the house. My booted foot squeaked on the steel floor. I froze. No sounds came from the house. I crept forward, now more careful about my shoe. My cybernetic foot's fake skin made no sound on the floor. Doc knew how to make quiet cybernetics, even if it took me a while to learn how to sneak with my new foot.

My cybernetic eye adjusted to the darkness. I had to turn my head to scan the room since my real eye might as well have been closed. The only light came through the open door and a small window.

The room I stood in had a coat hanger with various fur coats. Were the winters bad here?

I reached for a coat. My stomach clenched. I couldn't steal stuff unless I really needed it.

A leather pack hung next to the coats. That I needed. I grabbed it and peered inside. A bit of dried blood stuck to one compartment while another had some sort of pellets. I sniffed one of them. Most likely, they were livestock food. The blood encouraged me. If someone hunted, they'd have a weapon.

I grabbed the bag and tiptoed into the next room, which had a few chairs and a cupboard. Beyond that, blackness engulfed a doorway. A rifle of some sort hung on the wall over the cupboard.

I lifted it off the hooks holding it and worked to figure out the foreign technology. It seemed like the weapon had a very similar design to the Ordained weapons I was familiar with. Where were the bullets? A slot in the bottom of the rifle gave me the feeling it was unloaded. I hung it back on the wall and began poking through the drawers. I needed ammunition.

The first drawer had a leather-bound book with small text in a strange language. It could have been a Bible, but without being able to read it, I couldn't tell.

I opened the next drawer. A pistol lay within it. Magazines of ammunition lay beside it. I fiddled with the pistol and managed to remove the magazine. I pulled a bullet from the magazine and examined it. Hard metal made up the entire thing. No needle poked from the tip of the bullet.

My hands shook. This bullet was made with one purpose, to kill.

I reloaded the pistol before stuffing it and the ammunition into the bag. Dad had taken me hunting a few times. I could kill animals.

A wave of loneliness engulfed me. Tears clouded my eye as I searched for the ammunition for the rifle. It would serve me better hunting than the pistol.

My steel leg knocked against the cupboard.

Something moved beyond the dark doorway.

I scrambled from the room and through the next one. I made it into the open night air. A few animals chirruped.

I hurried to the *Deathhorn* and stuffed the leaves from the bales into my bag. Once I had enough of those, I crept to the kitchen and grabbed some bread, dried meat, and sacked water. I hefted the now-heavy bag over my shoulder and crept off the ship.

I walked to the edge of our huge ledge. The mountains shimmered in the light of the silver moon.

I searched for any sign of Human habitation. I needed to make it away from this settlement and to one where pirates weren't welcomed.

My cybernetic eye picked a glow reflecting off one of the peaks far up the valley. My real eye couldn't see it.

I headed in the direction of the glow. If my geography was right, the glow was to the southeast.

I found a path wide enough for a small vehicle. I hurried along the path toward the other settlement.

The night wore on, and my stolen pack's straps cut into my shoulders. I pressed on, even when my real leg ached with exhaustion.

The eastern sky lightened as I traveled.

Wind blew from the west. I stopped and lowered the bag to the ground, then sat on a steel boulder. I grabbed a sack of water and drank. My eyelid sagged. Maybe I could rest here for a little while.

Distant thunder echoed off the mountains. White clouds tore across the sky. The mountains blocked any hint of what chased the harmless white clouds.

Hadn't Klate said the storms were dangerous?

I finished my water and picked up the bag. With the threat of a storm, I couldn't rest.

I took off at a fast walk. My real leg ached. My thigh, where my real flesh met steel, throbbed.

Wind roared overhead. The mountainside sheltered me from the worst of the storm, but it still set me on edge.

Rain fell from the now-gray clouds.

The temperature plummeted. *Should have taken the coat.* I pushed myself into a slow run. Lightning cracked. The clouds kept darkening and the rain came faster. Hail joined the rain.

The sky above blackened. Now, it reminded me of a space battle hidden by black smoke. I'd never seen clouds so dark.

The mountain path spread into a ledge with trees and grass. I ran toward the back of the ledge, my gaze searching frantically for any sort of shelter.

A huge door took up part of the cliff face that towered above me.

A gust of wind drove me to the ground. I climbed to my feet and pressed on. I made it to the door and spun the strange knob. The door opened inward. I bolted into the room and shoved the door closed.

Blackness engulfed the room. My cybernetic eye detected a bit of light shining under the door. It did nothing to cut through the blackness.

I ran my hand along the wall until I came across some sort of switch. I flipped it.

A dim light in the ceiling beat back the darkness. The room was large enough for a small hover. Nothing adorned the walls of the room. Because of the high ceiling, I guessed the room was built to contain livestock. A smaller door stood in the back. I walked toward the door. Puddles of water marked my trail.

I threw it open and flicked the switch upward. Another light illuminated this room. One wall held rows of metal cans. Pictures on the cans hinted at their contents, which appeared to be food and not fuel. A large barrel sat on a cabinet in another corner. A spigot jutted from the bottom of the barrel. Folded blankets lay on a shelf next to a bare cot.

I opened the cabinet. Clean, dry clothes lay inside. I took off my own dripping outfit and put on the smallest set of dry clothes. They felt scratchy but better than something wet.

I sat on the cot, which was large enough for at least two Humans. This place appeared to be some kind of storm shelter.

Outside, the storm's roar increased. Even the thick metal of the mountain couldn't block it out.

The outer door flew open. For a second, I assumed the storm did it, then Klate strode into the room and shook himself, spraying water everywhere.

He led a gigantic bird after him.

I scrambled to the back of the second room and yanked the pistol from my bag.

Klate moved to duck through the second doorway.

I aimed the pistol at him. "Get out."

Klate's ears flipped backward, showing tension, but not stiff enough to show anger.

"I said get out!" I kept the pistol aimed upward at his hairy chest.

Klate released the bird's reins. "If I go back into that darkstorm, it will kill me sure as a bullet."

"I don't care." My finger touched the trigger guard. If I had my own stun pistol, I'd have shot Klate instantly.

The pistol's weight fought against my hand, the lethal bullets making the thing feel like it weighed twice what my own pistol did.

"Are you doing this for justice or revenge?" Klate's voice came out low and carried no hint of anger.

The pistol trembled in my grasp. *Vengeance is mine, says the Lord.*

"You murdered Dad," I snarled. My finger hovered over the trigger. Killing him would rid the galaxy of a dangerous pirate captain.

"We both know it was an accident." Klate's lips curled back. "When is it justified to kill someone for a mistake?"

"I'm not letting you sell me." The words came out high and frightened.

"Sell you?" Klate's ears flipped upward. "Where did you get that idea?"

"I heard you." *Shoot him,* part of my mind pleaded. "Tenned wanted to pawn me off."

"He thought we'd have to pay someone to take you in." Klate's ears drooped a bit, more sad now than angry. "We wouldn't spend that much on cybernetics if we intended to sell you."

I lowered the pistol slightly. "So you're not going to sell me?" My gut told me he wasn't lying.

"No. Think what you will about me, but ask yourself, would I have braved this storm if I only thought of you as something to pawn off?"

I let the pistol fall to my side. Klate's actions only made sense if he told the truth.

Klate held out his huge hand. "Give me the pistol."

I aimed it at him again. I didn't want to shoot him, but he couldn't have my only weapon.

Klate charged.

One swipe of his gigantic hand batted the pistol from my grasp. It skittered across the floor and under the cot.

Klate's hand came back, ready for a second swipe. I closed my eye and waited for the killing blow.

It never came.

I opened my eyes. Klate stood over me, his ears perked in their usual unreadable position.

Outside, the storm howled.

He hadn't killed me. He wasn't even mad.

Klate knelt and pulled the pistol from under the cot. He stuffed it in his belt, near his other pistol. "You couldn't have shot me anyway. There wasn't a round chambered." He pointed to the bed. "You can have the bed. I'll stay out there with the bird."

"How did you find me?" I demanded. "Did you use that chip you put in my head?"

"That chip can't be controlled by anyone but you." Klate's ears twitched. "I figured you'd go for the nearest settlement, so I borrowed the bird and headed after you. I hadn't expected you to run on a planet you'd only been on for a few hours, let alone make it this far. Your dad trained you well."

My jaw clenched. What would Dad think of me now, trapped with a pirate I couldn't kill? What about my looks? I was an ugly cyborg with the wrong number of fingers and toes. Some hunter I was.

A few tears dripped from my real eye. I stumbled to the cot and sat, then wiped it away.

Klate's ears drooped. He came to the cot and sat next to me. "It's okay to cry."

I sniffed. This time, I couldn't stop the tears or the sobs that followed.

Klate put his damp arm around my shoulders. I didn't resist. It reminded me a little of Dad, even if Klate's arm was huge and hairy. It still had warmth, warmth I hadn't felt since the grenade, and even if I didn't want to admit it, I needed his comfort.

Klate held me while I cried.

CHAPTER SEVEN
Departure

I stepped off the *Deathhorn* and onto the pavement of Tupra's biggest spaceport. Klate and Melsha followed after me.

Gray clouds hid the sky, covering the sun, asteroids, and moons I knew were above. From what I knew of Tupra, the clouds rarely lifted enough for the locals to see their wondrous night sky.

"You're sure you don't want us to take you to Saddat?" Klate asked. "You might have more luck finding your family there."

I hefted a pack Klate had given me. "They travel around." I hadn't mentioned that my "family" consisted of Akar and Reva. They made a lot of their coin hunting pirates and smugglers, not the middle-rung criminals Dad and I had hunted. Klate wouldn't like the idea of me joining with the elite hunters.

"I'm not sure if I'll go with them anyway. We had differences." I added. Dad had always turned his brother and sister down when Akar offered to let us join his team, even though we could have used the extra coin from the larger bounties. Sure, they were Loyalists like us, but from what Dad told me, they'd sometimes take their beliefs in obeying the Ordained almost far enough to disobey the rest of the Bible.

"Wait!" Doc darted down the ramp. He grabbed my cybernetic arm and pulled a small tool from his pocket.

With a few quick flips, he opened my cybernetic hand and began fiddling with the controls in it. He wiggled a few bits around, then closed my hand up, leaving only a thin crease in the gray skin.

"Unsheathe your claws," Doc said.

I stared at my fingers. Claws? The cybernetics didn't even have fingernails.

"Think of them as another joint in your finger." Doc bent over and began messing with my cybernetic foot. "They're actually needles, much like my own claws. They'll inject paralysis serum into someone. It's the same kind as in your darts so it won't work on Chix." He spoke fast, obviously proud of his creation. "They'll need refilled after two uses. Open the back and fill the little vials." His tail twitched, as usual. "Your hands can hold more venom than my claws, so you only need to inject two claws worth for something human-sized."

I focused on my hand and tried to unsheathe the claws.

A claw pierced the fake skin of my finger and swiveled into place. I stared at it. "Why didn't you just give me civilian cybernetics?"

Doc finished with my foot. "I don't do that sort of trash. My cybernetics are art. They should be displayed with pride, not hidden away. Your nose also has a filter in it that should give you a bit of resistance to some gasses."

"Why didn't I know about this?" I retracted my claw.

"Tenned didn't think we should let you have any weapons on the ship," Klate said. He pulled a small pistol and holster from a pocket in his pants. "Figured you might want this back."

I took the pistol and pulled it from the holster. It was the one Klate had taken in the Comet's Tail. Six stun rounds sat in the magazine. "Thanks." I put it back in the holster and attached it to my belt.

Melsha stepped past Klate and engulfed me in a hug. "We'll miss you."

I returned the hug.

She stepped back. "Sure you don't want to join the crew?"

I shook my head. "I'm not a pirate."

Behind Melsha, the rest of the crew stood, waiting to come down the ramp. During my trip, I'd learned most of their names. Tenned stepped past them and came to stand next to Klate. His red eyes were narrowed, as usual. "If you ever try hunting us, I will not hold back."

Klate ignored Tenned. "Melsha's right. If you do ever want a job, I'd be open to letting you on as a crew member."

I doubted Tenned approved of the offer.

"Thanks, but I'll be fine on my own." Even if Klate and Melsha got along with me, I doubted the rest of the crew would appreciate a hunter in their numbers, even if some of them were nice to me. Besides, I couldn't help them rob Ordained ships. The law was the law.

I craned my neck upward to meet Klate's gaze. "I forgive you."

Klate smiled a little. "Thank you."

If Tenned had killed my father, it would've been different, but Klate had shown he was sorry. I looked over the pirates one last time. They worked together like a family. Klate and Melsha would've taken me in, but the others? They'd never trust a bounty hunter. "Goodbye." I turned and strode through the spaceport.

A humid breeze blew, but my thick clothes blocked most of it.

I examined the ships in the spaceport. Unlike the *Deathhorn*, these had wings similar to a swallow. They were Tupra ships, manufactured on planet. Their unique looks made them stick out enough so that landing anywhere other than the black market towns of Lokostwa would be difficult, but the sleek predatory blackness of those ships would put fear into the hearts of anyone they attacked. A few other ships had Ordained markings. Were they Ordained ships or smugglers disguised as Ordained?

With Tupra having a large supply of flexsteel and bendsteel, perhaps the Ordained encouraged trade, even though they officially had an embargo on Tupra.

A huge wall circled the spaceport, but a set of double gates stood open. I headed toward them. The wall had the appearance of something meant to keep people in the spaceport. It might not be any good during a war, but it probably cut down on smugglers and hunters.

Two Elba guards stood at the gates.

My hands broke out in a sweat.

The shorter one, who still towered over any normal sized Human or Skallan, stepped toward me.

I froze and resisted the urge to drop my hand to my belt for the pistol.

"Where you from?" he asked, his Tupran accent thick. So far, he showed no obvious aggression, other than his ears being turned slightly back. All my instincts told me to be careful with any creature who could gut me with a single swipe.

"I came on the *Deathhorn*," I said.

The Elba's ears swiveled forward. "You know Klate?"

I nodded.

He glanced at the *Deathhorn*. "Good man, Klate." The Elba stepped out of my way. "Have fun."

"Thanks." I walked past the two Elbas and into Trader Town.

My mind ran over the information I knew about the place. Trader Town was the biggest known pirate haven anywhere near Ordained space, and judging by the two guards, pirates were well-respected here. Back in the Lokostwan town, the Ordained could have sent in an army of mercenaries if things got bad, but here, anyone who got in trouble was on their own.

Even though the Ordained militaries couldn't take the native planet of the Elbas and Varsillian, they had managed to destroy most of the government system, leaving Tupra in a state of what could best be described as peaceful anarchy where only the larger towns had any kind of governing system. Most of the religion on Tupra was of the Free Kin sect, with Loyalists being a persecuted minority.

The two guards were likely some sort of primitive border security meant to keep an eye out for anyone from the Ordained who tried infiltrating Tupra. The wall wouldn't hold up to a battle, but it gave them some idea of who landed in the spaceport.

Coral-like trees and pillars of every color and shape towered above the stores that competed for the attention of spacefarers. The first thing I needed to do was find somewhere to spend the night. With the cold humidity, I couldn't sleep outside.

I passed a row of stands selling fruits, dried goods, and meat. The smells set my stomach growling. I walked to the nearest one where an Elba roasted six-limbed creature of some sort over a fire pit made from spaceship parts.

Juices from the creature dripped into the flames, which flared with every drip. Did Tupra have six-legged vertebrates or was this an import from Korska? It was about half the size of a kark, small enough for someone to handle but big enough to feed a large family.

A young Elba peered from behind the strange bird-thing. "You want some? One bendsteel coin for a leg." She spoke Spacer well, though she had the Tupran accent. Her gaze landed on my cybernetics.

I pulled out one coin and handed it to her. Not a bad price, considering Tupra produced so much bendsteel. Maybe she felt sorry for me, or it was past whatever time people ate here.

She ripped off a leg and wrapped the end in a leaf before handing it to me.

I took the meat and bit into it. It carried a sweet taste and had been sprinkled with various kinds of seasoning. "It's good."

"Is there anything else I can do for you?"

"Do you know of a place where I could spend the night?" Tomorrow, I'd figure out what I wanted to do with myself. Going back to Ordained space would be the best option, but if I was on Tupra, I might as well learn about it. After all, not many hunters were brave enough to hunt on Tupra.

The Elba's ears twitched. "My aunt runs an inn down the street. It's called the Moonshadow. They've even got an opening for a dishwasher. I will warn you, Inissan has no clue how to cook."

"Thanks." With Tupra's cold dampness an inn would be worth whatever I had to pay.

I headed down the street. The amount of Elbas around set me on edge. There were so many of them. Though most were smaller than Klate, they were still huge. I prayed none of them would realize I was a hunter. Then again, with such a low rank, they might not care.

I passed three with red tattoos that looked like a knife, symbolizing murder. Most likely, they'd been tattooed murderers for killing Ordained soldiers in the Tupra War. Dad had disagreed with the Ordained when it came to the punishment of soldiers.

I found the inn, which had extravagant murals of comets, moons, and planets covering the whole outer wall. Whoever had painted them was an amazing artist.

I walked through the inn's doors. The inside walls were painted blue with clouds, asteroids, and moons. Unlike the tavern on Lokostwa, this inn had a homey feel with no dark shadows and the smell of cooking meats and roots had no dirt scent mixed in.

"Can I help you?" A female Elba with a graying muzzle stepped from behind one of the tables. She held a rag in one hand and a tray in the other. Other than her, the place was empty.

"Are you Inissan?"

"That's me."

"I'm looking for a place to stay," I said.

Inissan had white inner ears and her coat had just enough brown that I could make out the stripes.

"I can provide that. It's ten coin unless you stay ten nights then you get the room for nine coin a night." She ran her rag over one of the tables. "Do you know how long you'll be staying in these parts?"

"Not really." I looked at my feet.

"You're not from around here, are you?" Inissan stopped washing the table. "I'm guessing Saddat, judging by your accent."

"You're right." Of course, my accent would give me away, especially to Elbas with their sharp ears. Hopefully, no one would expect me to speak Tupran. At least everyone in this town seemed to know Spacer.

"What's your name?"

"Krys Karzil." I mentally kicked myself. I should have used a fake name. Then again, what were the chances someone on Tupra would know the Karzils were hunters? "I'll take ten days if you don't mind."

The Elba smiled. "Works for me." Her words were soft, much like Klate's.

She left the rag and tray on the table and went to the counter. She pulled a door key from behind the counter and handed it to me. "Up the stairs, first door on the left."

"Thanks." I walked up the stairs and to the door. I inserted the door key into the hole and twisted it. The door swung open, exposing a small room with a clean bed. Another door led to an even smaller room for hygiene.

I locked the door behind me and sat on the bed. I began sheathing and unsheathing my claws. Every time I did it, the action became more smooth and natural. The same went for my foot.

Klate had given me enough coin to get by for a while, but I'd need to find a job. What could I do? Other than hunting, I didn't know a trade. The Karzils had enforced Ordained law for generations, but a girl hunting on her own wouldn't last long.

I took off my dirty clothes and climbed between the covers of the clean bed. I'd worry about my future in the morning.

The next morning, the sounds of patrons dining awoke me. I climbed out of bed and got dressed. My clothes would need to be washed soon. I ran through a quick exercise regimen before leaving my room.

I took the stairs one at a time, still a bit unsure of my cybernetic leg, at least on stairs.

The room, which had been empty before, only had two free tables. The diners were mostly Elbas, but a few Varsillian sat at the tables. With serpentine bodies, they moved like swaying trees. As they spoke to each other, their colors shifted with their emotions. The shifting colors made it almost impossible for a hunter to get a positive identification on them. Luckily, they rarely left Tupra.

Inissan scrambled from one table to the next, a stack of plates in one hand and a rag in the other. Her ears were flipped backward. From the way she acted, I guessed she had to be close to panic with all the customers.

She hurried past me.

A plan entered my mind. "Do you need any help?"

"Do I ever." She tossed me a rag. "The Elba family in the back is about to leave. When they do, clean off their table, then go and wash dishes. If you work today, I'll give you a free night, and your food will be on the house." She pulled another rag from her dress pocket. "We've got a crew coming in."

The five Elbas exited the building. I ran to the table and began washing it clean of the grime it had accumulated from the dining Elbas.

Eleven Elbas, some with tattoos staining their fur, strode into the inn. A Gorkam hopped after them. Behind him, or her, four Torfs and two Varsillian came. They were all armed with pistols. A few had rifles. Two of the Elbas sported cybernetics. An old black warhound limped after them. I hurried behind the bar and began scrubbing dishes. I tried to ignore this crew, or at least look like I was. Smugglers rarely had over ten to a crew. These were pirates, and the various tattoos on their cheeks told me many were escaped slaves.

Inissan scrambled to take orders from the pirates.

A female Elba with reddish fur dipped her head respectfully to Inissan and ordered the food. By watching the way the crew looked at her, I guessed she was the captain. The warhound sat at her side. My fingers itched to take out my datsheet and see who the pirate was. She had a bold red tattoo on her cheek, but a long row of deep claw marks ran through the number. The scar seemed old, but it had been a hard blow. Judging by the size and distance between the marks, she'd faced down another Elba. Why did she have a pet warhound? Warhounds were especially bred for the Chix cavalry. That breed of kark wasn't something an Elba would own.

A family of four Skallan left and headed for their rooms. I washed the last of the plates and hurried past the Elba captain to the family's table. I grabbed a pile of plates and darted toward the kitchen.

The Elba watched me.

I deposited the plates in the basin and grabbed a rag to clean the table. As I walked past the Elba, I looked away from her.

Her huge hand darted out and grabbed my cybernetic arm. "This is military grade," she said.

"Let go." I tried to pull away from her, but she held on. Every claw but her trigger finger's claw and thumb claw were long and sharp, telling me she favored close range fighting. By the look of her scars, she'd been in many fights against things with claws and teeth. "Inissan, where'd you get your help? I don't like her looks."

I reached for my pistol.

Inissan hurried to the table. "Let her go." The words came out as a low growl.

"She's probably a hunter. These cybernetics aren't civilian." The pirate released me. "Word gets around that the Moonshadow's employing a hunter and you'll have no customers."

I held my cybernetic arm close to my body.

Inissan's golden gaze landed on me. "What ship did you come in on, girl?"

"The *Deathhorn*," I said without hesitating.

"Tell me who their cook is," the pirate captain said, her green eyes narrowed.

"Melsha," I said. It was a clever question. No info on the datnet connected Melsha to the *Deathhorn*.

Inissan watched me. "So, you're a pirate then?"

I shook my head. "I'm not really anything. Klate gave me these cybernetics after the accident. I'd rather not talk about it."

"They do look like Doc's work." The pirate's gaze softened. "Go back to work. Sorry for frightening you."

For the rest of the morning, I scrubbed the tables. By noon, most of the diners had cleared out. The ones who came in for the food had gone back to their ships while the ones who stayed in the rooms were exploring the town. Best I could tell, most of the people who stopped by were either smugglers, pirates, or tattooed criminals looking for work, though there seemed to be a few Tuprans who came to this port town to do trading.

I touched my pocket. Where was my datsheet?

I glanced around the kitchen, my eyes searching. That datsheet had a copy of my license on it.

Inissan leaned against the wall, her back to me. I stalked toward her.

She turned, exposing the datsheet in her huge hands.

I snatched it away.

"You are a hunter."

I couldn't tell what her emotion was. "I'll leave if that's what you want."

"You can stay. I know an orphan when I see one." She looked away. "I was one too. Got pretty good at picking pockets."

"Who was the pirate captain?" I asked.

"That would be Savora. She's a war hero in these parts, same as Klate. After the war left Tupra, she never stopped fighting the Company. She won't sell slaves unless she captures a hunter."

Very comforting. I began washing another load of dishes. Other than running water and a few perital tanks to fuel a generator, there was no power in the building. Probably a good thing, considering power would mean no job for me. I could work here for a while, but eventually, I'd have to go back to hunting. Here, I was nothing, just a dishwasher who didn't make any difference. In Ordained space, I'd been able to bring criminals to justice.

A dark sable Chix strode into the inn, her tail held high. "I want an order of narna flavor tilla worms and they'd better be alive."

Inissan's ears flattened. "You're not allowed in here, Nerrini."

I stared. Nerrini Kazini, the Chix that Dad and I had been hunting when I met Klate. Of course, this town, being the biggest spaceport on Tupra, would be where she'd go. It was the perfect place to bring in black market slaves.

Nerrini glared. "I happen to know where your niece plays. I suggest you get me my worms."

Inissan growled. "That threat might work with others, but not me. Your body wouldn't be hard to hide. Get out."

Nerrini flicked her tail tip downward in a rude gesture then strutted out of the inn.

"Sometimes, I wish more hunters came here and took care of those types." Inissan glared at the doors. "I wouldn't mind if she ended up dead in a ditch somewhere."

"You mean there's not enough of a law to lock her up?" I asked.

"Trader Town's security won't go after someone based on Company intel. We all know Nerrini's scum, but since she's never been caught here, there's no way to arrest her, not legally."

"So you do have some law?" I finished one of the plates and set it aside.

"There's a town council, mostly made of veterans. They keep the scum pirates out of town, deal with serious crimes, and the slave trade. We're on our own with anything that's not likely to turn into a battlefield. It's better than being ruled by a greedy company that only rose to power because they got a monopoly on space travel."

I ignored her barb at the Ordained and scrubbed a pot. "Is there work for someone who used to hunt bounties?"

Inissan shook her head. "They wouldn't trust you. Besides, bounties aren't a big thing here, and you'd end up dead in a hole first time you had to deal with an angry Elba. If you've got no family, it's pretty easy to go missing."

I went back to the pot. Though Tupra seemed stable on the surface, it hid a dark underside, one that ended with the less popular types buried in shallow graves. I'd have to be careful here.

CHAPTER EIGHT
Hunters

I walked down one of the narrow streets and hefted my pack a little higher on my shoulders. In spite of their huge size, Elbas never left much room to move about. Probably something to do with being a tunneling species.

With it being Sabbath day, few trading stalls were in operation. Most of the ones in operation were either run by non-natives, who viewed the Sabbath as falling on some other day, or by those who didn't believe in celebrating it. I examined the stalls as I passed them. With the little coin I'd earned from Inissan, I could afford to do a bit of shopping.

I eyed one clothing stall with a Varsillian manning it. It flashed light green. If my studies served me right, that flash meant this creature had identified himself as a male.

"These are fireproof." The Varsillian owner had a voice that sounded like wind through trees. He poked at a gray shirt and matching pants that looked something like a uniform. He had quite a few sets of these clothes. The set he pointed to would fit me.

I stepped closer. "How much?"

"It's fifty coin for the whole set. Good deal if you ask me. It could save your hide, or what's left of it."

I winced at the price. It wasn't a bad deal, but I needed to save my coin. "Maybe another time."

I wandered through the streets until I came to the edge of town. The bright colors of the coral-like trees stood in stark contrast to the boring gray sky. Birds and other small creatures darted through the trees. They grew into twisted, gravity-defying shapes enabled by their extremely strong but light fiber, and were as tall as the massive jungle trees on Chibbink, if not larger.

I left the city behind and ventured into the trees. A few himples stalked smaller creatures above me, their bright colors blending well with the multicolored vegetation.

I sat on a fallen coral tree and listened to the bird songs. With all the work I'd put in at the Moonshadow, I hadn't had time to stop and think.

Something large darted through the trees.

Remembering my training, I didn't turn to look at the shadow, but my gaze followed it. It zipped behind me. I turned my head slightly, not toward it but enough my cybernetic eye could pick it up.

Nerrini perched in the shadows of thick coral tree foliage, her dark fur blending perfectly. If it hadn't been for my cybernetic eye, I'd have missed her.

I kept my face turned away from her. She was a threat and I had no backup. In the trees, she had the advantage. Considering the things she'd been criminalized for, she hadn't come after me for a friendly chat. More than likely, I was the best way to get back at Inissan.

I couldn't walk back to the town with her above my path, so I walked deeper into the forest. Maybe I could get around her and make it back before she realized what I was doing.

Nerrini darted behind me where I couldn't see her without making it obvious. I kept walking. Part of me wanted to run back to Trader Town, but a plan formed in my mind. For all Nerrini knew, I was just some dishwasher. She had no idea I was a competent hunter, unless my cybernetics tipped her off.

Coral crackled above me. I kept walking without changing my stride. After a few more steps, I turned toward Trader Town.

My hand moved toward my pistol. I forced it away. I couldn't let her know she didn't have the advantage of surprise.

She sprang through the trees above, putting herself between me and Trader Town.

I couldn't play dumb any more.

I dove for a tree. A stun dart tore past my ear, slammed into the tree, and sparked against the coral bark. I ducked behind the tree and drew my pistol.

Nerrini scurried through the branches, making herself a hard target. She must have holstered the pistol.

She leaped into the tree above me.

I turned my body so my metal side faced her, giving me some protection from the darts.

Nerrini dove at me, her wing skin guiding her fall.

I stepped back and aimed upward. My real foot caught on a root as I backpedaled. I fell on my rear.

Nerrini landed near me and leaped for my throat, her claws ready to inject me with their paralysis venom.

I grabbed her throat with my cybernetic hand and extended the arm to its full length.

She choked and clawed at my arm, but her claws did no damage to the cold steel.

I brought my pistol up, shot her at point blank, then dropped her twitching body to the ground. I dug through my bag until I found a pair of cuffs and some rope. I yanked her hands behind her back, cuffed her, then tied the rope around her feet to hobble her. Now that the fight was over, my real hand shook so much it made the job difficult, but I got it done.

Nerrini growled and tugged against the rope. Being a Chix, the paralysis serum from my dart had no effect on her, but the shock from the dart had given me the time I needed.

"You're caught," I snapped. I kept my gaze on the trees around us. She might not have been working alone.

Nerrini glared at me. "Where do you think you're going to take me, girl?"

"Saddat." The shaking in my hand had subsided.

Her eyes widened, sending a thrill through me. I'd captured a dangerous bounty on my own. Now, I had to figure out how to get her on a ship to Saddat.

After a moment of thought, I dragged her to the nearest small coral tree, which was so wide I couldn't wrap my arms around it. I tied her to the tree then unraveled a bit of rope and used it to gag her. I couldn't risk hauling her through town, not without help.

I took off at a run for the Moonshadow.

By the time I got there, the sky had turned from gray to black.

Inissan met me at the door. "What's your hurry?"

"Nerrini tried to kidnap me." I gasped for breath.

Inissan's ears flattened. "I'll gut that little beast."

I chuckled. "I've got her tied to a tree. I'm not sure how to get her off the planet."

"What's the bounty?"

"Four thousand in coin." It would be enough money to get me elevated to point seven, not a good rank but better than what I had. "Can you get us both off Tupra?"

"I know at least a quarter of the smugglers who trade in this town," Inissan said. She scratched her chin. "I know the *Rogue's Way*, *Skycrusher*, *Warhound*, and *Samaritan* are likely to be leaving town this week."

"The *Samaritan*?" Could it be the same ship that had saved my parents and me over a decade ago? "Does it have a Torf captain?"

"Stakku and his wife have been captains for decades. Did you know them?"

"Sort of. I was a baby. The lightshields on the ship Mom, Dad, and I were on went down. That crew saved them."

Inissan smiled. "Then they'll be a good one for you to buy passage on."

The minister placed a bag of flexsteel coins on his desk and began fiddling with his own datsheet. "We'd been looking for this little piece of pitbait for years. Good work, Krys." His hair had gone gray with age, but he still had coiled muscles, hinting he'd probably been a bounty hunter before getting a less dangerous job.

"You should have killed me!" Nerrini shouted from her cell.

I ignored her and grabbed my new license from where it lay on the table.

Nerrini kept shouting. She'd done it the whole way to Saddat. I'd gotten a good look at her record. If anyone deserved to fight and die in the pits, it was her. Even the old Torf captain of the *Samaritan* hadn't complained about me taking her bounty, or threatening to starve her until I got the information I needed.

"Thanks for the coin." I stuffed it in my pack. "Are there any jobs around here?" If I could get stable work hunting local low-end bounties, the kind who paid the fine instead of being punished with slavery, it would be a lot safer. Those bounties rarely shot back, and I might even get a wage for enforcing the law, rather than depending on the bounties alone.

The minister shook his head. "Sorry. There aren't any towns around here willing to employ teenagers, at least not ones of your rank."

I frowned. It wasn't a surprise, though it was a bit of cruel logic. No one wanted a kid, which meant I'd have to get by on my own.

The minister's face softened. "Are you any relation to the other Karzils hunting here? There's a group led by Akar, then a couple more led by Madok."

"Akar's my uncle," I said. Madok must have been some other Karzil that was no relation to my family. "Thanks." I stepped out of the bounty ministry and headed down the streets of Saddat's capital. I'd find my relatives if I got in trouble, but right now, I wasn't ready to face that. They enforced the law like Dad and I had done, but sometimes, the end justified the means for them.

Shops stood on either side of the paved road, which was wide enough for large hovers. Unlike Tupra or even Lokostwa, these shops were indoor businesses big enough to employ others. The buildings around me had clear, domed roofs signifying that they were all upper-class buildings, not those belonging to the lower classes. Those would be near the edges of town, places where bounties sometimes hid.

I passed the buildings and paused by one of the many trees. Finally, I'd returned to a land of blue skies and rolling prairies, as well as an open city with room to walk on the streets and grass around the buildings.

I sat in the soft grass under a tree and began thumbing through the list of bounties in the area. Nerrini had given me some decent info about a few of her associates who helped with illegal slave trafficking. These weren't some poor children who got caught stealing bread. They were traffickers who needed to be taken off the street. This was the job I was meant for.

I thumbed through bounties until I found Jarkan, a Skallan. His bounty came in at five thousand, enough to propel me out of the points and into the single digits. Once I got there, I could license my cybernetic accessories or get them replaced with something more Human. I'd still need to make forty-thousand more in a year to get elite rank, but at least being in the single digits would be enough to get me taken seriously.

The problem was, Jarkan was a Skallan on Saddat, his native planet. This would make him hard to find. His only distinguishing feature past his facial structure was a tiny scar under his eye. That had kept him safe from most hunters, but I knew where he did his business.

I closed my eyes and thought. From what Nerrini told me, he liked to travel by night, which probably did a good job of hiding his features.

Night came fast on Saddat. Once darkness fell, I put on my jacket. It hid my cybernetic arm. As long as no one realized my cybernetics were overpowered or contained claws, I wouldn't have any trouble with the law, but it was best to be careful. Savora had shown I looked like a hunter or a pirate. Right now, looking like a pirate might be a good thing.

I consulted the map on my datsheet. After memorizing the narrow alleyways in what Nerrini said was Jarkan's neighborhood, I pulled my hood up and began walking.

The streets of the capital went from wealthy businesses to the poorer part of town where the roofs were simple and triangular, without the transparent domes, though many of these buildings still had skylights. Most likely, there wouldn't be that much violence here. After all, hunters spent a lot of time in the region. It had just enough crime to be good for hunting.

Then again, Jarkan had slipped by the hunters.

I headed down one of the alleyways. A Skallan stood at the end of it. Patches covered her worn clothing, but she stood tall, not like a beaten down slave.

I stood to my full height and turned, keeping my real side shadowed. "I came to pick up the stock," I said. Hopefully, the cybernetics would look pirate enough to make her think I lived on the edge.

The Skallan's golden eyes narrowed. "We don't deal in slaves here."

"Oh, sorry. Must have got the wrong alleyway. Barrok isn't going to be happy with me if I'm late." I'd picked up that name while interrogating Nerrini. "Do you know where Jarkan is?" I shifted from foot to foot, then stopped the nervous habit when I caught myself doing it.

The Skallan stiffened like I'd expected. "I'll get Jarkan." She sized me up as she touched a datcom on her wrist. To own that, she had to be well-funded. She looked at the door of a nearby building.

The door swung open and a large Skallan stepped out.

Behind me, something scampered along the rooftops. Most likely, Jarkan had a Chix bodyguard with a sniper rifle.

What had I been thinking, getting into this mess?

"What do you want?" Jarkan asked.

I controlled my breathing. I needed to pull this off, at least until I could escape. "Barrok's looking for stock," I said. I hated the word "stock" to describe slaves. They might have been criminals, but they weren't animals.

My cybernetic eye spotted the Chix, who stood in the shadows, a rifle in his claws. No other guards made themselves visible. Most likely, the Chix thought I couldn't see him in the darkness.

Jarkan waved his arm and stepped away from me. He'd seen through my act.

The Chix lifted his rifle.

I ran toward Jarkan and drew my pistol. As I charged, I turned and fired three fast shots at the Chix.

The Chix went down. I turned my pistol on Jarkan and fired a shot into his chest. The dart bounced off.

He drew a pistol.

I dodged to the right and reached for his throat.

A dart slammed into Jarkan's neck. He fell in a twitching heap.

I scrambled from the alley and darted around a building corner that would make decent cover. The female Skallan was still on the loose somewhere. Had she been aiming for me and shot Jarkan?

A dark Torf stood across the alleyway. I aimed my pistol at him.

His feathers shot up. He aimed his rifle at me. "Hunter?" he asked.

"Yes," I said.

"Then point that thing somewhere else." He lowered his rifle.

I pointed my pistol at the ground and peered around the corner.

The female Skallan had vanished. A woman stood over Jarkan while a man bound the Chix on the roof. The man climbed down with the Chix.

"You get him?" Another man, this one about five years older than I was, stepped from the shadows. He had a bit more fat on him than any serious hunter would ever have.

"We got him," the older man said. He dropped the cuffed Chix from his shoulder and bent to examine Jarkan.

He had a red beard that dropped below his chin like two tusks. Was it Akar?

"Jarkan's mine," I said. My voice squeaked a little.

"We'd been tracking him for weeks," the younger man said. It had to be Urkot, my useless second cousin.

"And I got to him first." I strode past the Torf and to Akar. "I want my bounty."

Akar smiled and patted his pistol. "It looked to me like he had you, girl."

I glanced at the woman. Reva, my aunt.

"You don't know who I am, do you?" I turned so he could see the right side of my face.

"Nope." Akar cuffed Jarkan.

"I'm Krys." The words came out in a sob. Even Akar couldn't recognize his own niece. The realization hurt more than I'd thought it would.

"Krys?" Akar hurried toward me and grabbed my chin. He gazed at my face. "It is you. I thought the pirates got you. Where's Brok?"

I instinctively stepped away from Akar's touch. "He didn't make it." I tried to keep my emotions under control.

The Torf and Urkot stared at me.

"How'd you get those cybernetics?" Reva strode toward me. She had a slight limp, one Dad told me she'd received during the Tupra War.

"The pirates. They thought they could get me to join their crew. It didn't work." Didn't she care about her brother being dead?

"Sounds suspicious." Reva folded her arms across her chest. She kept her red hair tied back and high on her head. "Did you get any info? It would help if we knew their hideouts."

"No." I looked away. "I don't want to talk about it."

"Leave the kid alone," Akar said. "She's been through a lot."

"So, do I get my bounty?" I still needed that bounty, needed to get my rank up.

"We'll give you two thousand then divide the rest between ourselves," the Torf said.

Reva glared at the Torf.

"You only get a thousand if you strike out on your own again." Akar watched me.

I seethed at the manipulation, but what choice did I have? Dad wouldn't have joined them, but I was alone. That fight with Jarkan could have gone bad in a hurry. I needed backup.

"Who's this?" I nodded to the Torf, one of the darkest I'd ever seen.

"Qwalm." The Torf dipped his head. "It will be a pleasure to have you on our team."

"Nice to meet you." Qwalm had been the one who offered me more coin from the deal, more than Reva had.

Reva grabbed the Chix, who had recovered from the shock of the stun dart. Jarkan was still paralyzed so Akar grabbed his arms. "Well, get his legs, Urkot."

Urkot scrambled to do as he was told.

Reva pulled out a datsheet. By the solid way it folded, it had to be the latest model. She scanned the Chix's face. "This guy's only worth a hundred."

"Save an image of his face and leave him," Akar ordered. "We'll say he got away and report his crimes, but add evading the law to the list."

Releasing low paying criminals until they turned into high-end threats wasn't right. What kind of people were my family? Then again, it was a random guard, not a true threat. Perhaps he'd been doing his job and didn't deserve years of slavery for his actions.

Reva released the Chix, who scrambled up the side of a building and out of sight.

I watched them, wary. Qwalm stood a bit taller than I, but with his dark feathers, he cut an imposing figure. Anyone who knew how lethal Torfs were at close range knew better than to mess with them.

We walked to the bounty ministry and handed over Jarkan. My license ticked upward two points to a point nine. If only I'd been able to take Jarkan on my own. *A thousand more coin and you'll be there.*

We walked through the ministry's doors and onto the dark street. A few stars reflected off the domed glass roofs of the high-class buildings.

"Do you have a place to stay?" Akar asked.

"It's warm here. I can sleep on the streets." Dad and I made it a practice to not waste money on comfort.

"We've got a hotel. You can stay there with us," Akar said. "I don't want you on the streets."

"I guess." A bed would be nice, and safer when I was alone.

I followed the four to their hotel. The white building stood tall. A glass dome covered the top. I'd never been in one of these hotels. When we stayed inside, Dad and I always picked the lower end ones.

I stepped through the door and onto a plush rug. The walls were painted white, and the lighting on the walls reflected off the glass dome above.

"This way." Qwalm bobbed his head toward one of the hallways. He wasn't as imposing under the lights.

I followed him and the others. At the end of the hallway, there were two doors leading to two separate hotel rooms. The walls went all the way to the high glass ceiling, leaving way more head space than we needed, a costly building style.

"We've only got four beds so I'll let you take mine," Qwalm said. "I'll sleep on the floor between you and Reva. Akar and Urkot sleep in the other room. They snore." He opened the door.

I walked into the room. Two huge beds stood on either side of the room. Another fluffy rug lay between them, one that Qwalm promptly lay on.

I poked the bed. "If you want, I could take the floor."

"That thing's a bit soft for sleeping." Qwalm twisted his neck around so his chin lay on his shoulder.

Qwalm was right about the bed. It took me half the night to fall asleep in it.

CHAPTER NINE
Outlaws

A week later, we managed to track down another bounty, a Skallan who had embezzled money.

"Krys, stay with Urkot. Only come if we need help." Akar ordered.

"This guy's not known for violence," Qwalm said. "Give Krys a chance. See how she does."

Akar's green eyes narrowed. "I don't like it. She's just a kid."

Qwalm's feathers lifted a little. "You saw her drop the Chix. If Jarkan hadn't had that armor under his shirt, he'd have been hers too."

"Fine," Akar sighed. "I'll let her go with you. Keep an eye on her."

Reva only watched. Maybe she didn't care if I got hurt.

Qwalm bowed his head to Akar.

Akar spread his datsheet. "Qwalm, block the back door. Krys, you go in. You'll run him straight to Qwalm. The rest of us will surround the building."

I'd get the bounty before Qwalm had a chance to take him. Akar and Reva needed to know I wasn't a dumb kid.

Qwalm and I walked toward the building. It made sense to send us. After all, we were the two least suspicious members of our team. Torfs, being mostly of the Free Kin sect, rarely became hunters, so Qwalm wouldn't draw suspicion. With Akar and Reva's heavy muscle and lean bodies, their looks screamed "hunters." My cybernetics set me apart, but I was young enough to get by.

Without a word, Qwalm left me and strode toward the back exit of the office building our target worked in.

I paused. Akar would have given me a quick chat, something about what I'd meet in the building, but Qwalm hadn't. Had he forgotten, or did he expect me to know what to do?

I stood tall and strolled into the building.

I walked past a few civilians, then took a flight of stairs, which creaked a bit more than I liked, even if I was trying to walk casually. A Human stood at the top of the staircase. A stunner pistol hung on his belt. A guard.

I looked at my feet. "Um, do you know where doctor Keesh is? I've got a package for him." I'd learned the doctor worked on the same floor.

"Keesh hasn't worked here for a year." The guard reached for his belt.

I drew my pistol and shot him in the neck. He fell to the floor, his hands twitching.

"Sorry. I've got work to do." I hurried past the guard. Next time I made up a cover story, I'd need to make sure my information I found on the datnet was up-to-date.

I burst through the second door on the left. Our target ran for the exit.

I fired.

The Skallan fell, a dart buried in his back. I winced. I'd been aiming for his hip. *Akar doesn't need to know that.*

I grabbed my folded datsheet and spoke into it. "Qwalm, I got him."

Soon, I heard clawed feet bound up the exit's stairs. Qwalm stepped through the door.

"I see you got the guard too. Good work."

"Is the guard okay?" Sometimes, the stun darts led to complications.

"He'll be fine." Qwalm bobbed his head. "You're a better hunter than Akar and Reva give you credit for."

"I'm not that good."

"You draw the pistol faster than most. Not quite Akar or Reva fast, but you're no rookie." Qwalm tried to pull our captive Skallan to his feet.

I grabbed the guy's other arm and helped Qwalm lift him. We dragged him down the stairs, his feet thumping on every step, then out past the civilians, who watched but steered clear of us. Once we were out of the building, Akar met us at one of the local hovers. "Good job, kid," Akar said. It made me feel warm, knowing he'd actually recognized my abilities.

Reva waited in the passenger seat. "I see Krys didn't get herself shot." Reva smiled at me.

Qwalm's crest shot up. "Of course she didn't."

Once in the hover, I sat in the back, while Qwalm had to put a seat down so he could crouch. I glared at Akar, Urkot, and Reva from behind. Why was it that Qwalm was already more of a friend than my relatives? Best I could tell, they'd taken me in because they didn't want me on my own, but they resented having to let me join them.

"How'd you get in with these three?" I asked Qwalm.

Qwalm rubbed a clawed hand over his feathers to straighten them. "Allied to go after a gang and stuck together afterward."

Urkot glared back at us. "I'd be an elite if it wasn't for you not giving me my fair share."

"Your fair share?" Akar laughed. "If you weren't with us, you'd have about as much luck surviving as Krys."

I clenched my steel fist. *I'd do fine on my own.*

"So, after we dump this guy off, would you guys like to go to a bar?" Akar asked.

"Sure," I said. Dad and I had made some easy hits where people tended to get drunk and forget they were hunted.

Akar squinted at me and shook his head. What was up with him?

Reva laughed a little.

Akar pulled into the ministry. We prodded the prisoner in. He glared at us, but kept quiet.

"Four thousand," the minister said. "How's that divided up?"

"Give Krys a thousand," Qwalm said.

"But that's not fair," Urkot whined.

"She shot him," Qwalm said. "Besides, she's the only one who hasn't reached the single digits."

"Thanks," I whispered to Qwalm while we got paid. A thrill shot through me. I'd made ten thousand in the last year. Now, I was a true hunter, not a kid living in someone's shadow.

We left the ministry. Akar drove through town until he came to a bar. He parked our hover a fair walking distance away like any smart hunter would do. With such a streamlined and shiny vehicle, we couldn't afford being seen near the bar, not when criminals might recognize it as belonging to someone who had coin.

"So, who do I pair up with?"

Akar stared. "Pair up with?"

"I didn't think we wanted to all go in together."

"Relax." Akar turned the hover off on our vehicle and it sank to the brick road. Akar stepped out and headed for the bar with Urkot following close behind. He strode toward the pub, more focused than I'd ever seen him. Surely he wasn't excited at the prospect of sitting in a pub and trying to find a bounty.

We walked into the bar together. Maybe being in a big group would make us less suspicious.

The interior of the building could have used more lights. We came through the door near the bar, which ran along half the length of the room. Tables stood a short distance from it, and another door opened near the tables, allowing patrons to leave without passing a bunch of drunks.

I eyed an empty table in one of the corners. Without even looking for bounties, my four associates headed straight for the bar.

Qwalm stood while the other three sat on stools. Akar said something to the Skallan bartender, who hurried to get drinks.

"Come on, Krys." Akar smiled, more laid back than I'd seen him since we met.

I slunk to the table. "Shouldn't we be looking for bounties?"

Akar grabbed some sort of alcoholic drink from the bartender. "Tomorrow's the Sabbath. We can sleep in."

Urkot downed a glass of something clear and held his hand out for another. "Haven't you ever gone to a bar just for the fun of it?" He started on his second drink.

I'd never eaten out without looking for bounties. Buying food or drink from a place like this had been out of my price range.

Qwalm took some sort of pink wine and sipped it. He slid a second small glass of the stuff my way. "Have some."

I sniffed it. It seemed to be some sort of fruity wine. I took a small sip. "Not too bad." I glanced around the bar again, instinctively looking for bounties.

Qwalm was already on his second glass.

I sipped mine while the others swigged their drinks. Qwalm didn't gulp his down as fast as the three Humans. Urkot drank like he'd walked through a desert. Whatever my Human companions consumed, they had the look of stronger drinks than the berry wine.

Akar wandered off to talk to a smoking Skallan with muscular arms and a pistol at his side. Probably another hunter.

"Do you want more?" the bartender asked me.

Dad's words came back to me. *Drinking's fine, as long as you don't get drunk.* "Some water and a bit of targan roast." Normally, I wouldn't have bought such expensive food, but I guessed my family would be paying.

The bartender brought me water and meat. I ate and scanned the crowd while the other hunters drank.

A group of six Skallan sat around a table in a dark corner, a place I'd have chosen if I picked the tables. I looked away from them.

Out of the corner of my cybernetic eye, I saw them shooting glances our way.

I grabbed the next glass of wine the bartender passed to Qwalm. "Don't look now but we're being watched."

Qwalm yawned. Alcohol made Torfs drowsy but didn't impair their judgment, unlike my other companions.

"A plate of roast broshoots, please." Qwalm slid the wine to Urkot, who downed it.

The bartender brought the food and some water. Qwalm ate and drank. Every once in a while, he glanced around the room, checking to see where our stalkers were. He bumped Akar and whispered to him. Akar waved his hand and guzzled another drink. Akar's drunk gaze landed on me. "So, who was it who murdered Brok? Was it the *Deathhorn's* captain or a crew member?"

I froze. "I don't want to talk about it." I wished the distress call Wurrud made before we were boarded hadn't made it through. That would have allowed me to pin the blame on a different crew, one who deserved it.

"*I* want to talk about it," Akar slurred.

Qwalm yawned again.

Urkot fell off his stool. Akar and Reva watched him stupidly.

"Time to go," Qwalm said.

"Can I have a sack of cold water to go?" I asked the bartender.

He handed one to me.

Akar and Reva lifted Urkot and dragged him through the door. Qwalm stumbled after them, his eyes half shut.

"I'm driving," I said.

None of my companions responded.

As we rounded the corner of the bar, two Skallan stepped in front of us. I recognized them as two from the pub. One carried a knife. The other had no weapons.

Qwalm stumbled past me.

Using my cybernetic hand, I held the water sack over his head and squeezed.

The sack burst, showering Qwalm with icy water.

His eyes snapped opened. He shook himself.

"We've got company," I said.

Akar released Urkot and fumbled for his pistol. Reva held on to Urkot.

Four Skallan ran up behind us. One tackled Akar.

"Hand over your coin and you won't get hurt," The one with the knife waved it in the air.

I reached for my pistol.

The Skallan with the knife charged. His blade slashed through the air.

I threw up my cybernetic arm. The knife clanged against my arm and slid off it, slashing toward my stomach. I dodged to the side.

The other Skallan charged Qwalm. Two more leaped at him from behind.

The knife wielder circled me.

Qwalm screeched, a wild sound that pierced the night. One of the Skallan leaped at his back. Qwalm kicked backward, catching the unlucky Skallan in the leg with his clawed foot.

I reached for my pistol. The knife wielder sprang at me, slashing and forcing me to abandon my pistol yet again.

I unsheathed my claws and swiped at the Skallan, dodging as I did so. My claws connected with his flesh. He stumbled away from me, his face bleeding.

Behind me, a stunner pistol popped.

The Skallan raised his knife too high. I sprang at him and my steel fingers closed on his wrist. I squeezed. Bones crunched under my hand.

The Skallan doubled over. I sprang away from him and drew my pistol.

Qwalm kicked his third attacker, downing him. The other two were already down, both bleeding from Qwalm's kicks.

Reva fired her pistol at the last standing Skallan. He bolted with stun darts flying past him. I aimed for him, but he ran around a corner and out of sight.

The other Skallan lay on the ground with a dart in his leg. In Reva's state, she'd been lucky to hit anything.

I checked my steel arm. A slight scratch marred its surface, but otherwise I was unharmed.

Qwalm helped Akar to his feet. Blood dripped from Akar's nose.

"Good job, Krys." Qwalm bowed his head to me.

"I should have been quicker on the draw." Good thing I'd had Qwalm.

"I got one of them." Reva's words came out slurred.

"You want to take them in?" I asked. The Skallan with the broken wrist fled down the street while one of Qwalm's tried to limp away. The other three hadn't risen.

Qwalm grabbed his datsheet and scanned their faces. "They're not wanted. I'll file a complaint. Besides, they're just drunk robbers."

I hadn't realized our attackers were drunk. Then again, Qwalm had a better nose.

Qwalm yawned.

Our attackers weren't the only ones who had too much to drink.

Our team made it to the car. I climbed behind the stick before anyone could complain.

Being unfamiliar with the hover, I had to drive slowly. By the time we made it to the hotel, my four passengers were asleep or passed out.

I shook Qwalm awake. He dragged Urkot to our rooms while I herded Akar and Reva. Akar's nose still bled. After how little help he'd been, I didn't care. I got them all in their beds, then settled into my bed.

No wonder Dad hadn't worked with Akar and Reva's team. Would it be better of I struck out on my own? I imagined going back to sleeping on the street and trying to bring bounties in on my own. It wasn't safe, not until I gained a bit more experience.

By the next afternoon, my team recovered from their hangovers.

"You want to spar a bit, Krys?" Qwalm paced the rug he slept on, his tail swishing. "You did well last night, but if you'd been fighting two people, they'd have got you."

"Sure." I'd been exercising regularly, but I hadn't practiced fighting enough.

Akar peered through the door. "Go easy on the kid."

I shot a glare at him. I wasn't a kid. *Lot of help you were in that fight,* I wanted to snap.

Urkot came into the room, probably wanting to see us spar. Reva sat on her bed and watched, her eyes narrowed, appraising me.

I turned my steel side toward Qwalm. He came at me and slashed with his clawed hand.

I blocked with my cybernetic arm.

He struck at me with his foot. I sprang back. Even my cybernetics wouldn't be able to take a Torf's kick. Qwalm kicked again.

I retreated.

"You've got to stop running away," Qwalm said. "You get backed into a corner."

"If I don't, you'll kick me."

"Then dodge like you did with the Skallan."

Knives were one thing. Huge clawed feet were another.

Qwalm struck at me. I tried to dodge, but his claws scraped against my cybernetic leg. I darted away.

This time, Qwalm didn't let up. He charged with his chin lowered to protect his throat and his claws upraised. *Never fight what you can shoot,* Dad always said.

The words did me no good. I threw myself sideways, onto my bed.

Qwalm sprang onto the bed. One of his feet landed on my chest, a blow that would've crushed ribs and torn my gut if he'd been fighting me for real.

Without thinking, I swiped at his leg with my cybernetic arm, catching both of them.

Qwalm squawked and tumbled from the bed. I pounced on him before he could rise, pinning him to the floor. I grabbed his throat with my cybernetic hand.

"Good job," Qwalm said.

Akar clapped. "Not bad, girl."

I released Qwalm. He rose and winced as he stood.

"Did I hurt you?" I stared at his leg. He'd taken it easy on me, but I hadn't taken it that easy on him. If he'd kicked instead of pinning me, he could have split me open.

Qwalm tested his leg. "It's only bruised. You did well. You're fast, but you need to stay on your feet."

"I think I'll shoot Torfs," I said.

Qwalm chuckled. "Good idea. Humans are bad at close combat. We'll keep training more whenever we have the chance."

He had a point. We Humans had no natural weapons, though I had a few unnatural ones from my time with the pirates.

"We'll do what we can to keep you out of the fighting," Urkot said. "You're not old enough to be a hunter."

I resisted the urge to draw my claws. Maybe Akar was old and experienced enough to treat me like a kid, but Urkot wasn't.

"Last fight I remember, Qwalm and I saved your drunk hide." I glared at Urkot. "I wouldn't mind seeing who's the better hunter here."

"Sure, kid." Urkot stepped toward me.

I readied myself. Qwalm had held back. Urkot wouldn't, but neither would I.

How much training did Urkot have anyway? He had studied at a hunter academy, but so had I. It all came down to what sort of experience he'd gotten outside the academy.

He strode toward me, his fists lifted.

I stood my ground.

Urkot experimentally swung his fist at me. I ducked the slow fist and punched him hard in his ample belly. He let out an *oof* of air and slapped a fist into the cybernetic side of my head.

Sparks shot through my vision.

Urkot kicked at me, a high kick aimed at my stomach.

I dodged back and tried to grab his foot. I missed. His foot grazed my stomach.

"You should give up." Urkot smiled.

I waited for him to attack. This time, when his fist swung, I blocked it with my cybernetic hand.

Urkot swung his other fist. It connected with my stomach.

I stumbled back.

Urkot advanced. I swung my real fist into his side, then followed through with my cybernetic fist to his chin.

Urkot fell. I pounced on him and grabbed his throat. I kept my claws sheathed. Something made me want to keep them a secret. "I win."

"Ouch," Urkot said. "Did you have to hit so hard?" There was a venom in his voice.

I let him go and backed off. "You hit hard too." I rubbed my stomach and coughed. I needed to do better next time, but I had beaten him. It wasn't luck either. He was slow, even if he hit hard.

"Keep practicing," Reva said. She still had her usual cold look. I'd hoped she'd be a little impressed with me taking Urkot on. "It's time we head to Lokostwa and show the freaking pitbait there that we don't take kindly to them messing with Karzils."

With the use of a slur to describe Free Kin, my taste of glory turned to a weight in my chest Maybe the criminals on Saddat deserved punishment for their crimes, but many of the ones on Lokostwa hadn't done anything wrong. It wasn't right to go after them to get revenge for what a few pirates had done by accident.

CHAPTER TEN
Cost

Because Akar, Reva, and Qwalm had elite status, they were able to get us to Lokostwa without paying for it. We disembarked from the civilian liner we'd taken and stepped onto the now familiar yellow dirt of Port City's spaceport. I glanced at the ships around us, most of which were freight ships, other than the line we'd come on.

"We'll split up," Akar said. "Reva, take Urkot."

"Why do I always get stuck with her?" Urkot whined.

"Because I've got the highest pay grade." Akar folded his arms across his chest and looked at me. "On second thought, Reva, take Krys. I'll take Urkot. Qwalm can go on his own. He'll get closer to Torfs that way."

I stiffened a little. I'd have preferred going with Akar. He treated me like a kid, but at least he wasn't hostile like Reva.

Reva grabbed my real arm. "Come on, girl."

I pulled away and followed her. We came to the busy marketplace. Most of the people milling about were Torfs or Gorkam. Because we'd landed in Port City, there were also Skallan, Humans, Chix, and an Elba or two.

Reva slid her fancy new datsheet into my hands. "Scan their faces. If one of them comes at you, I'll back you up. Don't go for anything less than a thousand, unless it's something from a pirate crew."

I nodded. *Just like with Dad.* I played the innocent child while the firepower backed me up. Then again, could I trust Reva to back me up if things got bad?

I darted through the crowd.

A light tan Torf wore a scarf that covered her cheeks. I held up the folded datsheet and scanned her face. The datsheet scanned so fast, and from a distance far enough that the Torf didn't see it happen.

Wanted for association with Free Kin radicals, the datsheet read. *50 coin.*

I moved on. One like that would have to be hauled to the local Ordained ministry and released if she paid a fine. I'd leave her for the local hunters who didn't have to worry about blowing their cover. It wouldn't pay to haul her to Saddat or Chibbink.

After scanning dozens of faces, the datsheet lit up on an older male Torf. *Free Kin Radical with known associations to terrorist cells. 1250 coin.*

I darted away from him and watched as he went about his business. Was this worth it? Melsha had been so kind to me, even though she had no reason to show kindness to a hunter, and her crimes had been similar. I moved on without taking the guy. I'd find someone else, someone like Nerrini.

A young Skallan darted through the crowd. This one had bright green scales and new clothes. He had to have coin. I followed him. It was entirely possible he was some business owner's kid, but it wouldn't hurt to scan him.

He weaved through the streets and hurried into a building. I peered through the building's dusty window. Guns hung on the walls. A Skallan his age who hadn't been through an academy couldn't legally own a modern projectile weapon. Not that people on Lokostwa cared about illegal weapons trade. I backed away from the shop and waited for him to exit.

After a short time in the building, the Skallan stepped outside. I held up the datsheet and scanned his face while he looked at something on the other side of the street.

Nazar, son of Otton, captain of the Nightslayer. *Wanted for piracy, thievery, murder of one hunter, slave trafficking. Crew member of the* Nightslayer. *Age 15. 6,000 coin.*

I tailed Nazar. As he walked, he began looking around more. A few times, his golden gaze moved past me.

I pretended to be interested in a stall selling some sort of rough gemstones.

A young Elba with red fur and black stripes stepped from one of the alleys. Nazar bumped shoulders with the Elba. The Elba stood taller than me but shorter than Akar.

The pair darted into an alley. I followed after them. They were trying to lose me before heading back to their ship.

I took stock of the weapons. Nazar had a pistol, but he could have hidden other weapons under his loose white shirt. The Elba had a long knife. He wore no shirt. I figured it was a safe bet he didn't carry other weapons, though his claws were sharp.

There were fewer people in the alleyways. They'd realize I hunted them, so I'd have to strike soon. *Is this right?* The two were both young, too young to deserve the pits. I wouldn't wish the pits on Klate, so why would I send these kids there? For all I knew, they might not even have committed the crimes listed.

A presence moved behind me. I turned, my hand on my pistol.

"How much are they worth?" Reva whispered.

Any hope of backing out of this vanished. "The Skallan's six thousand. I don't know about the Elba."

Reva licked her lips like she wanted blood, not money.

The pair walked around a corner.

Reva ran after them, her hand on her pistol. She bumped into a Gorkam, who scrambled out of her way.

I raced after Reva and we rounded the corner.

Nazar and his companion, who had only made it a few steps, spun to face us. Reva drew her pistol and fired. Before he could reach for his pistol, Nazar fell in a heap.

"No!" The Elba slammed into Reva. Her pistol went flying. A knife gleamed in the Elba's hand. The pair tumbled to the hard-packed dirt in a pile of fur and fury.

Reva twisted the Elba's hand and plunged his own knife into his shoulder.

With one arm, Reva blocked his claws then kicked the Elba backward. He fell to the ground and clutched his bleeding shoulder.

Reva scooped up her pistol and leveled it at the bleeding Elba. The knife, still in her left hand, dripped blood. I hadn't even see her pull it out of him.

"Stop!" I shouted. The Elba wasn't going anywhere.

Reva's eyes narrowed.

I hurried between her and the Elba, who barely looked at me. His face wrinkled in pain. Blood leaked between his fingers.

I pulled a bandage and tube of salve from my pack.

"Give me the datsheet," Reva demanded.

I handed her the datsheet. I eyed the Elba's belt. Did he have some sort of tracking chip like Melsha's?

Reva scanned the Elba's face. "He's an escaped slave, only worth two hundred. Must have dyed his tattoos. Leave him." Blood dripped from four long scratches on her arm.

"He's a person." I reached for the Elba's shoulder.

He growled.

"Move your hand," I said. "I'm trying to help." I held out the bandage.

The Elba let me peel his bloody hand away from the wound. The wound went deep but didn't appear to hit any bones. The bleeding could kill him before he'd have to worry about nerve damage.

I squirted some salve in the wound then wrapped the bandage around the wound. It was a smart bandage so it could tighten to reduce blood flow. Hopefully, it would keep the Elba alive. He lay still. I peered at the belt, but it didn't have a buckle or anywhere to hide a chip.

"I got two." Reva held the datsheet up to her mouth. "I might need backup. They're pirates."

I glanced at the Skallan. He'd fallen in a position so he saw what happened.

Within a few minutes, Qwalm arrived. "Looks like you had some trouble."

"Krys insisted on wasting a bandage on that thing," Reva snapped.

Qwalm lowered his head to me. It wasn't much of a bow, but it showed respect. "We'll take him to a doctor before we give them to one of the shippers."

Reva smiled slightly. "I've got a better idea. We use him to see if that Skallan knows anything."

"No." The Elba pushed himself into a sitting position. He swayed.

Reva grabbed his bad arm and yanked it behind his back.

He growled, more from the pain than anything.

Qwalm shoved Reva away from the Elba. "I'll handle him."

"Traitor," the Elba gasped. "No true Torf would ever side with the Company."

"Can you stand?" Qwalm asked, ignoring the accusation.

The Elba glared with eyes the color of spring sky.

Qwalm grabbed his good arm and pulled him to his feet. "If you don't want cuffed, you'd better behave."

The Elba growled. Considering he couldn't stand without Qwalm's aid, the growl wasn't very threatening, not when he couldn't have been any older than fourteen.

Reva and I hoisted Nazar between us and followed Qwalm, who dragged the Elba to some sort of hospital. From the look of it, it wasn't a very good one, not with the amount of dirt on the walls.

A Gorkam stood at the door. By its large size, I guessed it was a female. "Bounty?" she asked.

"Needs patched up." Qwalm helped the Elba into the hospital, which had a low ceiling and metal walls covered in rust. Dust covered the floor.

The nurse pulled off the bandage. "Clean wound." I couldn't read her expression enough to know if she sympathized with the pirates or not. She worked fast, applying a numbing gel, then gluing bits of the flesh together. She finished the operation. "Thirty coin."

Reva counted out the coin, using the less valuable bendsteel to get the correct amount.

By then, the paralysis was wearing off Nazar.

Reva cuffed Nazar and we headed for the spaceport.

Akar and Urkot met us at the edge, a spot we'd chosen where the locals weren't likely to congregate.

"How much?" Akar grabbed Nazar's chin and turned his head.

Nazar snapped at Akar, his white teeth flashing. "Hands off, hunter."

"Six thousand," Qwalm said.

The Elba glared at Akar. "I hope you think of the innocents you sent to the pit when you spend that bloody coin."

Nazar bumped his shoulder against the Elba's good one. "It's okay. We'll get out of this." Nazar's words came out confidently enough I almost believed him.

A chill shot through me. Was he expecting his family to rescue him like Klate rescued Melsha? At least this time, we'd be leaving our bounties with the shippers instead of escorting them to Saddat.

Reva shoved her way between Qwalm and the Elba. She grabbed him by his bad shoulder and threw him to the dirt.

He snarled in pain.

Nazar thrashed in Akar's grip. "Leave him alone!"

Reva crouched and prodded the Elba's shoulder. She used her foot to pin his good arm down, then looked at Nazar. "Tell me who you sell to here and I'll leave him alone." Reva smiled as she spoke, enjoying her control over the helpless Elba.

I tensed, anger burning in my chest. I'd threatened to not feed Nerrini, but I'd never take things this far and not with a kid.

Qwalm let out a low hiss. His hackles lifted slightly, telling me he sided with me on this brutality.

"Don't talk," the kid growled between clenched teeth.

Nazar looked at the ground. "It's in Darkmine. I don't know the dealer's name. Dad doesn't take me there." He looked at me. "Please, leave him alone."

"Any other pirates dealing with the crew?" Reva asked. She reached to prod the Elba's shoulder again.

"The *Starfire*, and maybe the *Deathhorn*. Really, I don't know much. Dad doesn't tell me enough."

Reva stepped away from the Elba. Qwalm helped him to his feet.

We walked down the dusty street to where the shippers were located. Two Skallan stood outside the closed hatch of a boxy ship. They both held rifles at the ready, leading me to believe they were guards.

"We're here to deliver two prisoners," Akar said.

The guards relaxed slightly. One of them spoke into a wrist datcom, similar to my datsheet but wrist-mounted. "We've got five hunters and two prisoners." He stalked toward us and scanned our faces, then scanned the prisoners.

"High bounty for a kid," the guard remarked.

The ship's hatch opened and a Chix stepped out, his head held high. "It's fifty to ship each prisoner," he said. "Pirates are double."

"When did that happen?" Akar demanded. "The Ordained pay you, not us."

The Chix grimaced. "They don't pay enough for hauling, not with pirates around."

"Fine," Akar snapped. "You don't get the Elba. We'll sell him at the local market."

"He's a pirate," Nazar said. "We released him from slavery. He's been with us ever since."

I stared. If the Elba was left on Lokostwa, he'd be forced into the mines. Elbas, being natural tunnelers, were more at home in the mines than any other species. If he was lucky, he'd even get released after a few decades. Pirates went to the pits. Was Nazar dumb enough to sentence his friend to death?

"He's right," the Elba said. "I'm a pirate."

The sparse hair on the back of my neck stood on end. *They're up to something.*

"Fine. We'll take both now and send you the extra coin if we can get the Elba convicted for piracy." The Chix's tail twitched.

"You'd better send us the coin." Qwalm's feathers stood up.

The Chix spread his hands. "We're gonna. What'd you think we are, pirates?"

The Chix handed us the bounty for the pair of prisoners, minus the transportation fee. As we walked away, my stomach tightened. Had I done the right thing? Those two were just kids and shouldn't be given red tattoos, but what if I'd doomed a crew of people to pirate attacks? I tried not to think about it. The Ordained knew how to deal with pirates. It wasn't my problem, but I knew Dad would never have been so brutal to a pair of kids, not like Reva had been. This was why we'd avoided them.

CHAPTER ELEVEN
Choice

The next day, we spread out to hunt while Akar went to see if the shippers would pay us more for the Elba.

I stalked the streets, trying to stay as far away from Reva as possible. If I found a bounty, I wanted to take it on my terms, not hers. I passed a few beggars and placed my hand on my borrowed datsheet, making sure they couldn't pick my pockets.

After hours of hunting and scanning faces so often I drew glares from those who spotted me, I scanned a black Elba. *Chakkon: crew member of the* Rockdodger, the datsheet read. *Wanted for piracy, murder of hunters, war crimes, illegal slave trafficking, and theft. 10,000 coin.*

I tailed the pirate, staying well away from him. He stuck to populated areas, areas I wasn't willing to start shooting in.

He had no tattoos, much like Klate, but he was a bit shorter and thicker in build, certainly someone I wasn't willing to take on my own. Akar and Reva would do it, and this guy was good coin.

The Elba paused. I turned away and pretended to examine graffiti on the wall.

He pulled a few coins from a bag on his belt and tossed them to a skinny Torf child. The Torf ran off.

He resumed walking. I didn't follow. If he gave beggars coin, I couldn't bring myself to shoot him. Who even knew if he was guilty of the crimes he'd been accused of? Even Dad rarely hunted people for war crimes. All that meant was the person took the wrong side in Tupra War, and if they were in the war, they often got classified as murderers for killing in combat.

I went back to hunting but had no luck finding any bounties, other than a few low-end ones that weren't worth taking in.

Reva and I headed back to the inn, where we met Qwalm and Urkot. We grouped together in the room I shared.

Akar stepped through the doorway, his clothing dusty as the rest of ours. "They're not paying us for the Elba. Those shippers were all pretty tight-lipped and jumpy. I'm guessing something happened."

"Pitbait!" Reva swore. "Any other luck?"

Akar's lips turned upward slightly, which raised his mustache. "I looked into Darkmine and got a message from one of the local hunters. There were a few slave ships pirated last week, so there might be pirates in the region. From what I know, *Deathhorn* attacks slave ships most of the time." Akar flipped the screen to show us the bounty on Klate's head, sixty-thousand. "It's time to get revenge."

I prayed some other pirates were in the area and not Klate, but Akar was right. The ship in the area was most likely the *Deathhorn*. Klate's tactic of attacking slave ships and releasing the slaves had become predictable. Other pirates might have attacked slave ships, but Klate was the one who specifically targeted slave ships that had little in the way of valuables.

"Shouldn't we pick easier targets?" My mouth had gone dry.

Urkot, who stood behind Akar, grinned. "With a bounty like that, we're going for it."

"I don't care if they scare you." Reva strapped on both her pistols. One had bullets. "We're taking him in."

"What are you doing with that?" I demanded. "Klate doesn't use body armor." Without body armor, piercer bullets were unnecessary.

"These are pirates. I can hold thirteen shots in this pistol. With a price like that, we'll still be doing good if we bring him in dead."

I backed away from her.

Reva shot a glare at me. "You got a problem with enforcing the law?"

"No." With shaking hands, I holstered my stunner pistol and checked my ammunition. Six rounds in the pistol and two extra magazines. I glanced at my bag. All my possessions were already packed, a habit I'd had since Dad and I often moved fast. I tried to keep my breathing steady. Would I be on my own again? I had enough coin to make it for a while. I could make it.

"You okay?" Qwalm tilted his head.

Akar slapped me on the shoulder. "This will be good for you. Qwalm, let us get our shots off first. Brok wasn't your family."

Would telling them the truth do any good? I looked at the wooden floor of our room. It was Klate's best chance. "Dad's death was an accident. Klate threw a fire grenade back after Dad threw it." I ran my real hand over the cybernetic side of my face. "The pirates saved my life, gave me these cybernetics, and treated me well while I was on the ship." I gazed at my hands, afraid to meet my family's eyes. "I tried to escape once, ran right into the middle of a storm. Klate risked his life to save me. When they left me on Tupra, they even gave me some coin."

Urkot snorted in disdain.

"Some pirates have strange moral codes. It doesn't mean they're not criminals," Akar said. "You might want to stay here until this is over. It sounds like you've got captive syndrome."

My fists clenched. Akar thought I'd become some weakling who started siding with her captors because they didn't beat her. Did he really think I was that weak-minded? What could I say to convince him and Reva? I met Reva's cold gaze. Nothing I could say would stop them. They wanted coin.

"You'll get over it." Akar left the room with Urkot. "Be ready for a hunt first thing in the morning."

Reva looked at me. "You're too much like Brok, never willing to go far enough to move up." She stepped out of the room.

I glared at the back of her head. *Better to be like Dad than like you,* I wanted to shout.

Qwalm watched them go before he turned to me. "Do you think you've got captive syndrome?"

I shook my head. "They never meant to hurt me. They let me go. I know how prisoners are treated, and they didn't treat me like one."

"I believe you." Qwalm glanced toward the other room. "Have a few family members who were on the bad side of the Ordained, even a pirate or two. Doesn't make them evil."

"How can you stand working with my family?" I asked.

"Figure I might be able to hold them back from killing someone," Qwalm said. "That's why I'll be going on this hunt." He checked his darts. Unlike Reva, he had no killing weapon, just a stunner rifle and pistol. "After this is over, how about you and I break off and make our own team?"

"I'd like that. Maybe we should break off now." If both of us left, Akar and Reva might decide it was too dangerous.

"I'm not leaving without warning." Qwalm fixed me with his green gaze. "You can do what you believe is right. Follow your own path, not what people push you toward."

I stared at my cybernetic hand. "I'm going with you," I said at last. If Reva went for the kill, I had to stop her. If only there was some way to warn Klate, but I couldn't think of anything.

"You hang back," Akar ordered.

I stopped. Ahead of us, a warehouse stood above the other clay buildings. A cold wind tugged at my jacket.

Qwalm and the others circled the warehouse. As soon as Reva, Urkot, and Akar were out of sight, I hurried to join Qwalm. He bobbed his head at me.

By my reckoning, Urkot and Reva both had pistols with bullets. Klate and any of his crew would be using stunners.

We circled the warehouse until we made it to a door. Qwalm pressed his head against it to listen.

"You're going to go through with this?" I asked.

"I enforce the law. I don't kill." Qwalm listened.

God, please don't let Klate be in there. I silently prayed. Maybe it was a different pirate, one who deserved to be captured.

"I won't help the pirates, but I'm not helping you either. I don't want anyone getting killed," I said.

Qwalm ignored me.

The pops of stunners erupted from the warehouse. Qwalm kicked the door open and aimed his rifle.

As my cybernetic eye adjusted to the dimness of the warehouse, I took cover behind a stack of rotting crates.

A Torf I didn't recognize dove behind another stack of dusty crates. Akar took cover behind a pile of bricks. Another Torf, not one of Klate's crew, lay still on the floor. I scanned the room for pirates. Judging by the direction Akar peered, the pirates were somewhere behind a pile of raw bendsteel.

Qwalm took a hurried shot at the standing Torf. She darted farther behind the crates.

Tenned peered around the pile of bendsteel and fired at Akar. Stun darts sparked against Akar's hiding place.

Qwalm fired at Tenned. Tenned fell in a twitching heap. My heart sank. We were up against the *Deathhorn's* crew.

There wasn't anything I could do to help him. At least it was Tenned, not Melsha or Klate.

Someone dragged Tenned behind the pile of metal, but from my angle, I couldn't see who it was.

"Got to get closer," Qwalm hissed. "Reva's blocking the front door."

The hidden Torf fired at Akar. I hadn't realized the Torf was armed.

"Give me cover," Qwalm ordered.

I drew my pistol and fired over the Torf's head. I could keep her from shooting back without actually hitting her.

Qwalm dashed toward the hiding place, his rifle upraised. Klate leaped from behind the rubble pile and fired at Qwalm. Qwalm tumbled and slid across the floor. Klate picked up Tenned and sprinted for the door.

I holstered my pistol and ran after Klate. Reva had to be stopped.

One of Akar's darts buried itself in Klate's shoulder. He fell to the floor with Tenned. Dust billowed around them.

No.

Klate rose from the floor and lifted Tenned to his shoulder. The Torf fired at Akar.

Klate stumbled toward the door, slower now that he'd been hit.

I sprinted for the door. I either had to stop him or stop Reva. Reva stepped through the doorway, one pistol in each hand. Next to her, Urkot lifted his killing pistol.

With a roar, Klate charged.

I leaped between them and turned on Klate. He came at me, his free hand upraised. I rushed him. At any second, he'd slash me with his claws.

Klate hesitated.

I slammed into him and dug two of my claws into his throat. We went down in a pile of fur, scales, and metal. A bullet cracked through the air over my head. The paralysis serum shot into Klate's bloodstream.

Klate's gaze met mine, his eyes sad. If he wanted to kill me, he had time before the serum kept him down. "I'd hoped you would have chosen a better path," Klate slurred. He relaxed under me.

I climbed off Klate and stood, my leg shaking.

"You almost got killed," Reva snapped.

"You almost killed him!" I yelled at her.

"Urkot fired that shot." Reva glared at Urkot. "What an idiot."

Urkot looked at the ground.

Akar limped across the warehouse.

"Where are the Torfs?" I asked.

"I got grazed by a dart," Akar said. "Just the jolt. The Torf got her friend and escaped while I was down. I doubt they were worth much." Akar knelt by Qwalm and injected him with a paralysis antidote. We all carried one, but they were expensive. Dad and I had saved ours for emergencies.

I pulled Tenned from under Klate's shoulder and got them both in more comfortable positions.

"You did good, kid." Akar slapped me on the back.

Good? I'd betrayed Klate. *It wasn't betrayal. You stopped Urkot from shooting him.*

"That was impressive," Reva said. "You should have shot him instead of choking him down. He almost gutted you."

"He hesitated." I stared at my feet.

"Urkot, get our hover," Akar ordered.

Urkot slunk out of the warehouse while Reva and Akar cuffed and disarmed the two pirates. Reva pulled two collars from her pack. She tightened one around Klate's neck then pushed a few buttons on it. I winced. The collars were made with a needle that pumped paralysis serum into the bloodstream, keeping prisoners paralyzed for hours.

Reva did the same to Tenned.

I rubbed my neck and imagined a long needle embedded in it.

Qwalm groaned. I walked around the bricks and warehouse trash then knelt by him. His legs scrabbled on the dusty floor, but he couldn't get them under his body. I helped him get his legs positioned. "Think I can stand," Qwalm said after a few minutes.

I helped Qwalm to his feet. Only then did I see the blood dripping from his leg.

"You're hurt."

"A scrape," he said. "Fell hard." His words were still slurred.

Urkot arrived with the hover. It took all three Humans to get Klate loaded. I held onto Qwalm and looked away.

"It's not your fault," Qwalm whispered. "You saved his life."

More like put off the inevitable. He'd be thrown in the pits for sure. Would he be one of the Martyrs who let someone else kill him, or would he fight back and become a popular attraction?

I tried to shove the thoughts down.

"Well, are you two coming?" Akar sat in the driver's seat of our hover.

I helped Qwalm into the hover and sat beside him.

While we drove to the shippers, I bandaged Qwalm's skinned leg. He'd lost a lot of feathers and skin, but the wound wasn't deep.

We made it to where we'd seen the shippers last time. No ship rested in their place. A sign directed us toward a building next to the spaceport.

Akar drove to the building and turned off the hover.

Thick bars covered the tiny windows of the brick building.

A Skallan met us. "If they're pirates, you guard any prisoners you lock here. After we lost the last ship, we're not doing pirates for such low pay. You'll have to find your own help to haul them to Saddat or pay the shippers more. There's another ship coming here in three days. They might take the risk."

"Pitbait," Akar swore. "Reva, when we get them in, you stay here with Krys."

I hung back while the others dragged Klate and Tenned into the holding cell. A little hope flared. If the pirates were getting enough power in this region to perform raids, maybe there was a chance for the crew. The opportunity wouldn't last long. If pirates got bold enough to raid, hunters and Ordained mercenaries would arrive soon.

Akar pulled out his datsheet and pressed a few buttons. He held the datsheet to his mouth. "This is Akar Karzil calling all hunters near Darkmine, Lokostwa. We believe the *Deathhorn* is in the region. We are going to strike when we get a team together."

I resisted the urge to pace. The *Deathhorn* crew couldn't rescue Klate if there were this many hunters. All I could do was wait.

Over the next hour, hunters began showing up. Soon, there were at least a dozen. Judging by their new weapons and datcoms on their wrists, almost all were elites. If Klate's crew was caught unaware, they wouldn't stand a chance. Melsha, Hirami, Doc, and the others would all be captured and sent to the pits.

Akar organized the hunters into search parties based on who had aircraft, though most were local high-altitude hovers.

I paced.

"I can fight. Leave Urkot here with Krys," Reva said.

Urkot glared.

Akar checked his ammunition. "I need someone here who can fight. There could be a rescue attempt, or someone could try to steal our bounties."

"And her?" Reva shot a glare at me.

"She did well with Klate. We've underestimated her. She'll be an elite in no time."

Before, praise from Akar would've felt good, but now it only drove the knife deeper.

Akar and the other hunters left in hovers. Some were high altitude hovers, which would make it easy for them to hunt down the *Deathhorn*. Akar took one of the other hunters' hovers, leaving Reva with our hover.

I had to do something.

Reva leaned against the wall of the prison. The bag sat beside her where she'd tossed Klate's numerous weapons. Klate's and Tenned's datsheets would be there.

A cold wind blew across the spaceport. I pulled my shirt tighter around my neck.

Reva folded her arms across her chest.

I waited and shivered. Any action I took would be going against the Ordained. In small ways, Dad had gone against them before by looking the other way for low-end criminals, but I'd be doing something huge. *God, give me wisdom*, I prayed.

"I'm going to get my coat." Reva hurried to the hover, her feet kicking up dust as she went.

I ran to the bag of weapons and grabbed the first datsheet I found.

Reva dug her jacket out of the hover and put it on.

I stuffed the datsheet in my pocket and stepped away from the bag.

Reva's eyes narrowed. She leaned against the wall and watched the horizon.

I thought of Melsha. What had she ever done to deserve the pits? The Ordained had made her into a criminal. My mind turned back to the Bible and what it said about following the law. Something within told me Klate's version was the right one. A just God wouldn't want me to serve evil.

I hurried to the hover and dug through it, pretending to look for my jacket. Instead, I pulled out the datsheet and flicked it to what I guessed was the *Deathhorn's* code.

"Krys to *Deathhorn*," I hissed. I turned on the video so whoever answered could see me.

"Krys, why are you using Tenned's datsheet?" The voice was a Human male, probably Ralkom, the mechanic.

"What are you doing?" Reva stomped toward the hover.

"The Hunters are—"

Reva grabbed my shoulder and yanked me from the hover. She threw me on the dusty ground and picked up the datsheet.

"Krys? What happened? Where's Klate?" the voice said.

Reva held up the datsheet. "You traitor." Her words were cold. She threw the datsheet in the dirt and brought her heel down on it.

I drew my pistol.

Reva kicked it out of my hand. "I suggest you surrender now, brat." Reva put her hands on her hips.

She didn't even consider me worth shooting. Rage built up in my chest. I sprang to my feet and slashed my claws at her head. She dodged backward, but I connected with her cheek.

A bolt of electricity shot through me. My muscles seized. I writhed in the dirt as sparks filled my vision.

Reva kicked me in the stomach. "I don't care if you are blood kin, you are dead." She holstered her pistol and sauntered to the hover, blood dripping from her cheek.

I lay still, the paralysis serum coursing through my body.

Reva came back with a collar. She tightened it around my neck. The needle plunged through my skin. I couldn't even whimper.

After she disarmed me, Reva grabbed my arms and dragged me into the prison. She dumped me next to Klate and locked the barred door to our cell. "Have a good time with your friends." She stalked outside but still within earshot.

"Akar, our little niece is a turncoat," Reva snarled. She paused, waiting for a reply from the datsheet. "No, I didn't kill her. I locked that pitbait with our prisoners. Don't tell Qwalm."

I lay helpless on the floor, unable to even turn my head to see my fellow prisoners. *God, please let the crew get the message.* They had to know something was up. They'd have a better chance than I had.

CHAPTER TWELVE
Cyborg

I lay on the hard floor and listened to Klate's and Tenned's breathing. Klate breathed slowly while Tenned's breaths came in ragged gasps. He was fighting the serum, not that it would do him any good. We were helpless, unable to do anything but wait for hunters to return and haul us away.

A hover hummed outside. Reva talked to someone, probably Urkot. The hover left, but the voices remained. So we were dealing with at least two hunters.

My neck throbbed from where the needle pierced it.

I clenched my cybernetic fist. This was so wrong.

I'd clenched my fist.

I unclenched it and tested my cybernetics. They moved easily, but my real body parts refused to respond. Somehow, my cybernetics had made it around the serum's neurological blockage.

I inched my cybernetic hand to the collar and ripped it off. The needle pulled loose. Warm blood trickled down my neck.

I rolled myself over so I could see Klate and Tenned. They were both facing away from me.

Using my cybernetic leg and arm, I inched across the floor. Bits of rock dug into my stomach and face, but I ignored the grit. I couldn't lift my head to escape it or use my real limbs.

I reached for Klate's collar. From my angle, I couldn't rip it off. I pushed the button that retracted the needle.

Klate's body blocked my path to Tenned. With only two working limbs, I couldn't make it over him.

I relaxed and waited for the serum to wear off. Blood dripped from my neck while my scrapes from crawling across the floor stung.

My life is over, I realized. I could never be a hunter, not now, after what I'd done.

Tears streamed from my eye. Even if I escaped, even if I saved the crew, I had nothing, no job, no family, no real friends. All I'd have was a bounty on my head.

After half an hour, my real limbs began responding though they were weak and sluggish. I crawled over Klate and to Tenned and then removed his collar.

I couldn't salvage my life, but I could repay Klate.

Klate rolled over. "Krys, check the door. See if you can get it open."

I crawled to the door. Bars ran up and down and braces ran across. They weren't overly thick. They hadn't been designed with an Elba in mind, but they'd most likely hold one. The hinges were old and rusted, probably a remnant from before the Tupra war.

I crawled back to Klate. "I doubt you could break it down. It looks pretty strong. If you try, Reva will realize we messed with the collars."

Klate closed his eyes. "We'll have to wait for them to take us out. We can get the jump on them then."

"Akar's got a bunch of hunters after your crew."

Klate's eyes widened. "How many?"

"At least ten."

Klate struggled to his feet and stumbled to the door.

I stood too. No need to pretend I was paralyzed with a huge Elba tromping around.

Tenned tried to rise but slumped back to the floor. "What side you on?" he slurred.

I opened my mouth to answer then closed it. I didn't have a side, not now.

Klate slammed into the cell door. It rattled but held.

Twice more, Klate slammed into the door.

"Hold on." I knelt at the base of the door and examined the hinges. "The hinges seem to be the weakest point." I reached through the bars and grabbed one in my cybernetic fist.

Using my cybernetics as leverage, I pulled on the hinge. Rust fell from it.

I jerked. The hinge bent. A slight crack ran through it.

"Reva, I hear something," Urkot whined.

Klate barreled past me and slammed into the cell door.

The bottom hinge sprang loose in a shower of rust.

Klate hit the door again. The two remaining hinges snapped. The door flew to the floor with a clang of metal.

Klate erupted through the hole, his hands upraised

Urkot charged into the room with Reva close behind. Urkot fired his stunner pistol.

Klate's huge hand slammed into Urkot's chest. He flew into the wall and slumped in a heap.

I charged Reva. She drew her killing pistol. A shot echoed off the walls of the prison. Something slammed into my upper leg.

Reva ducked around the doorway and ran.

I paused at the doorway. If I tried to go after her, she'd kill me for sure.

My leg throbbed. I reached down and felt the wound, expecting a small shrapnel wound or a bruise. My hand came back covered in blood. The bullet had hit me.

A hover revved up.

My injury could wait. I ran to Urkot. He moaned and opened his eyes. Blood soaked through four claw marks across his chest.

I relieved him of both his pistols. The killing pistol felt heavy in my cybernetic hand. I handed it to Klate.

Klate leaned against the cell, his body loose. He'd been hit by one stunner round, but it wasn't enough to take him down. "You okay?" he slurred.

I glanced down at the wound. More blood covered my pant leg. "I think it went straight through. I can walk."

Tenned climbed to his feet. He stumbled and fell on his side. "I don't recover like I used to," he grumbled.

Klate sank to the floor and crawled to Urkot's datsheet. He pushed it a few times then threw it to the floor. "Looks like they've jammed the whole region. We need to contact the *Deathhorn*." He looked at my leg wound. "Can you travel?"

"Yes." I peered outside. Reva was gone with the only hover. Could we get one from the city in time?

Klate glanced at Urkot's first aid kit. "Get your wound bandaged."

I grabbed Urkot's first aid kit and bandaged my leg. Without taking off my pants, I couldn't do a very good job, but I did squirt a little salve into it. The wound didn't hurt that much, but it did bleed quite a bit.

Urkot watched. From the way he clutched his shoulder, I guessed it was dislocated. The wounds on his chest bled, but not enough to kill him. He'd live.

"I hope you die in the dark," he gasped.

"You know Reva only keeps you around to draw fire?" I snapped. I didn't know if it was true, but considering how inept he was, I wouldn't put it past her. I turned to Klate. "What do I need to do?"

Klate pulled himself to his feet. "I want you to head due east. You need to warn my crew there's a whole army of hunters after them. They're by three peaks that stick out of the desert. They'll have their ships covered with camotarps."

I'd never known the pirates had access to the expensive tarps that could hide almost anything. Those didn't come cheap.

"Anything else?" I glanced toward the door.

"No. Go now. We'll make it out."

"Look for an antidote," I said. "Urkot probably has one." My leg throbbed. Maybe it was worse than I'd thought. "Be ready if they come back," I told Klate.

He nodded to me.

I limped out of the building and into the open. There were no hovers around. I jogged out of the spaceport and toward the cold desert.

After jogging for a few minutes, I spotted the peaks.

I headed toward them. They seemed to stay the same size, no matter how far I ran.

A rock caught my real toe. I fell in a heap. My head swam. Why was I tired already? I climbed to my feet and staggered. My leg throbbed, worse than before. I looked down at the bandage.

Blood soaked through and ran down my pants.

I ran on. If I didn't get medical attention soon, I could bleed out. Reva had taken my first aid kit, and I hadn't thought to keep Urkot's with me.

I pushed myself harder. I couldn't die without sounding the alarm. The crew depended on me.

By the time I made it to the peaks, they were only blurry outlines in my vision.

"Halt!" a distant voice shouted.

My real leg folded under me. Lying down felt better.

A humanoid shadow appeared over me. "What are you doing here?" It was Ralkom.

"Klate sent me. Hunters are after you, dozens of them." Darkness clouded my vision.

"She's losing blood. Get her to the infirmary now!" Melsha shouted.

My vision went black.

I awoke in the infirmary. Doc perched at my side.

Slowly, I pushed myself into a sitting position. My pant leg had been cut off and the wound on my leg now bore a bandage. Otherwise, my clothes were intact.

"I thought about giving you a matching pair, but the wound wasn't bad," Doc said. "Two cybernetic legs would be easier to deal with than one."

I shuddered. "If you're going to cut anything else off me, get my permission first."

Doc's tail twitched. "Fine, but keep it in mind."

I swung my legs over the bed and stood. The floor hummed underneath my feet, telling me we were in space.

"How are you feeling?" Doc asked. "I gave you a transfusion. You almost bled out. Don't ignore bleeding wounds like that." His tail twitched for emphasis.

"I'm fine." I tested my leg. It ached but held. "Are Klate and Tenned okay?"

"They're here. We picked them up, but the hunters are after us. They've set up ambushes. We're not sure where."

"Where are we?"

"We're in orbit over Lokostwa. They're narrowing down our location as we speak. Lucky for us, the ship detection tech here is pretty basic, so we're okay, until we take the engines past an idle, but we can't hide forever. We didn't get the *Deathhorn* restocked."

I gazed at the walls of the *Deathhorn*. If it came down to a fight, the old ship wouldn't hold out. "What are you going to do?"

Doc's tail twitched downward. "Klate's calling in favors, trying to see if others will help."

I hobbled from the infirmary, not sure where I'd go. I limped to the cockpit where Amellia sat. Klate stood next to her.

"You did well, Krys." Klate turned and crouched so his head was my level. "Thank you."

"We're being pinged," Amellia said. "I'll make a run for Tupra."

The ship's vibrations increased. We were on the run.

"Isn't Tupra the place they'll expect you to go?" I asked. My hunter training told me there'd be ambushes all along the routes to Tupra, and with the ship low on supplies and most likely, fuel, we couldn't afford to slow and turn, meaning we'd have to take a straight path.

"They will." Klate stood. "If we get close enough to Tupra, we'll have allies. I'll take the risk."

Was he gambling on the theory that we'd be boarded? It'd be better than getting blown up, but we'd be sent to the pits. I clenched my cybernetic fist. Maybe dying in an explosion would be a better way to go.

CHAPTER THIRTEEN
Showdown

I sat in my alcove and read some of the Free Kin Bible on my datsheet. We'd been traveling for two weeks without incident. Almost everyone but Klate and Amellia were trying to sleep.

This part of space was a sort of bottleneck between asteroid fields, the perfect place for an ambush. We didn't have the fuel to go the long way around, so we had to go through. The *Deathhorn* was already traveling at half-speed, in hopes the hunters would lose interest or assume we'd gone another direction. That was the only defense we had.

The ship jerked. I slammed into the front of my alcove and bounced around. The gravity glitched and the ship shuddered. We were coming to a fast stop, jerked from lightspeed by the reverse thrusters. The lights dimmed, then went out, leaving only glowing strips of paint to show our location. The gravity went completely down, but the ship seemed to have slowed.

I braced myself against the walls of my alcove so I didn't drift.

"Hirami, follow me." Ralkom flew from his alcove and grabbed a rail on the wall. He pulled himself from the room and through the hatch toward the cockpit.

Hirami bounded after him. The young Chix did a good job of navigating in zero-g. Had the crew been training him in my absence, or was he a natural?

Two of the other Torfs on the crew floated out too. I guessed they were the gunners.

The ship's vibrations were weak, not a solid hum like they should have been. Most likely, the hunters had used the pirate tactic of dumping debris in the ship's path, which overwhelmed the lightshielding and forced the ship to slow or be torn to pieces by space dust. Now, the engines had to cool down from the overexertion they'd gone through.

Tenned peered from his alcove. "Everyone, stay in your alcoves and keep the slides shut." He watched me as he said it, probably because the rest of the crew knew what to do.

Klate's voice came through Tenned's borrowed datsheet. "We'll be doing sub-light evasive maneuvers."

I braced myself in the alcove. The ship shuddered a few times, but with no gravity, I didn't get hurt.

The gravity flashed on. Klate's voice came through the speakers. "They've hit us with a hijacker. Get ready."

"How many?" Tenned demanded.

"A major Saddat bullet fighter and two more minors waiting."

I did a quick estimate. The major bullet fighters tended to have a crew of about thirty. The minors had around half that. The *Deathhorn* only had twenty, so we were going against three times our number if they all chose to board. Most likely, the minors would hang back and guard the major fighter from attack by enemy ships. If we were lucky, only one crew would board. Two ships trying to board a hijacked vessel at the same time was a risky proposition.

"Krys, stay in your alcove," Tenned ordered. "If things get bad, go for the ventilation ducts. They're designed to double as escape tunnels."

If the hunters won, they'd crawl into the ducts and drag me out, but it would be better than being in the alcove and getting hit by a fire grenade again.

"Is that clear?"

"Yes," I said.

If we lost, I'd be sent to the pits, same as the pirates. I climbed from the alcove. I needed to fight for my freedom.

Klate strode down the hallway, his ears flipped backward. He nodded to me and stepped through the hatch.

I took it as a sign and followed after him. I wouldn't cower in a hole, not this time.

Tenned glared at me but kept his mouth shut.

Doc crouched low. He knew better than to get shot when the crew needed a doctor.

Tapping echoed through the hold.

I drew my pistol.

"Stay in the hallway," Tenned snapped. Did he not trust me, or was he trying to keep someone he considered inexperienced from getting killed?

I stopped near the hatch leading to the hold and let the other crew members hurry past me. They spread out in the hold, using the cargo for cover, some hiding at the top of the stacks of supplies. The cargo had been arranged to give the pirates cover, a clever move on Klate's part. From my vantage point, I was above the hold, able to see down somewhat well.

"Open the hatch," Klate growled.

The hatch whooshed open. Hunters leaped through headfirst. Almost all of them landed on their feet, a hard trick considering the ships were belly-to-belly, which meant the hunters had to dive through a hole and then come upward through the *Deathhorn's* floor.

I took a few quick shots. One missed. The other hit a human in the chest. He stumbled but didn't fall. These hunters were armored.

Darts flew in every direction. A few sharp cracks told me at least one person had bullets.

Pirates fell. The hunters scrambled for cover, most of them never making it before they were hit.

The hair on the back of my neck stood on end. Something about the attackers felt off. Why were there so few hunters? Hunters and mercenaries didn't take huge risks like attacking pirates who outnumbered them.

A boot-step sounded behind me.

I spun, my pistol aimed at the movement.

Reva stepped through the next hatch in the hallway. A huge Elba stood behind her. More hunters followed. They'd hacked through the belly of the *Deathhorn* and come in without using a hatch. They must have done some sort of seal so the ship wouldn't depressurize.

The pirates were positioned to deal with the hatch threat in front of them, not enemy flanking them from behind and above. The attackers charging through the hatch were a distraction.

"They're coming!" I shouted to Klate. I had to stop them. I pushed the nearest hatch lever. The hatch doors whooshed shut, sealing me with the hunters. Only then did I realize I should've gone to the other side of the hatch before shutting it, but now, I didn't have time to open it and jump through. My best chance was to get in close.

I charged the hunters, trying to keep Reva between myself and the others. I fired at her. One dart hit her in her armored chest and the other flew wild.

Reva took aim. "Traitor."

I dodged.

A bullet split the air by my head. I fired at Reva. She leaped sideways. A dart bounced off my steel arm, one fired by a hunter behind Reva.

We collided. Reva kicked my legs out from under me.

I fell but grabbed her shirt in my cybernetic fist. She fell on me, driving the wind from my chest.

Reva grabbed my real hand. She slammed it into the floor. Pain shot up my arm. My pistol skittered across the floor. Reva aimed her killing pistol at my head.

I struck at her throat with my cybernetic hand.

She reeled backward and slammed into the corner of the open hatch.

I scrambled away from her.

The Elba, a big male with sandy fur and darker stripes, stepped toward me. He waved his long claws in the air. "Do you surrender, cub?"

My pistol lay near his clawed foot.

I stumbled to my feet and unsheathed my claws. "You're not getting through that hatch."

The Elba hunter chuckled. "How stupid are you?"

I met his icy gaze. "I prefer brave." I dove for my pistol.

The Elba swiped at me. His claws slammed into my cybernetic arm.

I hit the floor and rolled, but his attack had its desired effect. I didn't reach my pistol.

The other hunters behind the Elba stood back. They weren't going to come between an Elba and his prey, even if going around us would get them through the hatch.

The Elba stepped toward me, his walk slow. He knew I wasn't a threat. I had no hope of beating him, not without my pistol. I could bide my time. I grabbed my knife in my real hand. Pain pulsed up my arm. So Reva had broken my hand.

She lay still on the floor, her pistols out of my reach. Akar crept to her and started dragging her out the hallway.

The knife in my throbbing hand, I climbed to my feet.

The Elba stepped over my pistol. The only way to get it was to go through him.

I charged.

The Elba's claws slashed the left side of my head. I slammed into the closed hatch and slumped to the floor. Sparks shot through my vision then my cybernetic eye went black. I tried to rise but fell back to the floor.

The Elba crouched in front of me. He drew back his huge hand for the killing blow.

I lifted my knife.

The hatch whooshed opened causing the Elba to look up.

Klate, a storm of fur and claws, slammed into my attacker.

The hunter Elba backpedaled and slashed frantically at Klate.

It did no good. Eyes narrowed and ears flat against his head, Klate attacked in a flurry of claws, more like an unstoppable force of nature than a person. Sandy fur flew from the Elba's chest and throat. I crawled away from the two titans.

Blood spattered on my real arm. Klate's claws slammed into the Elba's chest, then another blow hit the side of his head. The Elba fell in a pile of blood-soaked fur.

Klate roared again, then pulled the rifle off his back and shot at the hunters.

Klate's crew charged through the hatch and fired at the hunters. The hunters retreated.

I touched the cybernetic side of my face. Three furrows cut through my replacement skin and to the metal underneath. Near the edges, blood oozed from places where the replacement skin covered flesh.

I tapped my eye. It stayed dark. I climbed to my feet. My head throbbed so I leaned against the wall.

Blood dripped from a claw wound on Klate's leg. He clutched his shoulder and looked at his crew.

I glanced at the crew, some of which hadn't come through the hatch. Almost half of them were missing. An old Torf named Falto and his sister lay on the floor. A Skallan lay near them, but the others I spotted were okay.

Klate removed his hand from his bloody shoulder.

Doc scurried through the hatch. He slathered Klate's leg in salve then climbed up Klate and did the same to his shoulder. He sprang off Klate and landed in front of me. "What sort of injuries do you have now?"

"My eye's not working."

Doc reached up and twisted my cybernetic eye. It popped out of my head. He fiddled with it then shoved it back in.

The eye switched back on. The image was pixilated, but at least I had some vision.

"Better?" Doc asked.

"It will work," I said.

Doc glanced at Klate. "Should I help him?" He pointed to the downed Elba.

"Go ahead." Klate stepped past the Elba and waved to the crew. "Come on."

I picked up my pistol and joined with the rest of the crew. We followed after Klate. He stopped at the next hatch, which had been closed. He pounded on it. "Will you surrender?"

"Never!" a Skallan voice shouted. "We outnumber you. Open that hatch and we'll use bullets."

Klate sighed. He pulled his datsheet from his pocket. "Tenned, where are you?"

"We've taken the hunter ship, but I'm down to five crew. Melsha is going to stay here to work out the hijacker bot."

"Tell me when you get to the hatch." Klate ended the call and looked at his crew and me. "I want three of you to get into the room using the ventilation system. We'll all attack at once. Hopefully, being attacked from three sides will be enough to get the hunters to surrender. Try to take out their leader."

"I'll lead," Likkil, the old Elba, said. She twitched her ears. "I can fit through the ducts."

"I'll go too," said Geshan, the blond Human.

"I'm going," Doc said. "It'll be close quarters. I'm good with those."

We needed one more. "I can do it," I said.

Klate's eyes narrowed. "Can you? You took a pounding."

My leg still ached from being shot. "I can do it." I switched my pistol to my cybernetic hand. My real one had started swelling. I switched back. The pistol felt wrong in my cybernetic hand. Maybe I had less control over it, or it was the fact I only had three fingers.

"You're sure?"

"I've got a bit of a headache, but I'm not in any worse shape than you."

"Then go." Klate limped to a grate on the floor and flipped it open.

Likkil crawled through the hatch. Though the ventilation ducts were designed for Skallan to use as an emergency escape route, she managed to fit down the hole. Geshan followed her. I went next. Doc darted in after me. Unlike the rest of us, he managed to walk on two legs, though even he had to stoop.

Likkil paused under the next grate. Her ears twitched.

I held my breath. Hunters paced above us, their boots echoing through the shaft.

Likkil held up all four fingers, made a fist, then held up her four fingers two more times, then held up two fingers. Fourteen hunters.

She grabbed the datsheet and punched a button. We waited.

Likkil tensed, her muscles bulging under her fur.

I got ready to spring forward.

Likkil burst through the grate. A hunter shouted. From the thump he made, I guessed he'd been standing on the grate when Likkil lifted it.

Geshan leaped out of the hole.

I followed right into the middle of chaos.

Hunters tried to dive for the sparse cover, but the sleeping alcoves were not meant to be used as cover in a battle. Others fired wildly, their shots bouncing off the walls.

Likkil leaped at a Skallan. Shots from a killing pistol echoed through the room. Likkil roared. The bullets did nothing to stop her momentum. She slammed into the Skallan. They went down in a heap with Likkil on top.

A Chix leaped at me, his feet leaving the floor as he came at me. I shot him. The electricity shot through him, stiffening his body and sending him crashing to the floor. Being a Chix, He'd be up in no time. Hunters and pirates fought, some shooting while others abandoned their weapons in favor of close combat. Klate charged into the room and threw a Chix across the room.

"Murderer!"

I spun toward the shout. A dart glanced off my cybernetic cheek.

Akar pulled his trigger again. His pistol clicked. He threw it to the side and drew a knife.

Behind Akar, Reva lay in one of the alcoves, her skin pale in death. I'd killed her.

"I didn't mean—"

"You'll pay!" Akar charged.

I stepped backward and aimed at him. My cybernetic heel caught on the Chix I'd stunned. The bullet wound in my leg shot a bolt of pain through me.

I fell.

A dart slammed into Akar's neck. He dropped next to me. I scrambled away from him, my pistol still in hand.

"Put your weapons down!" Qwalm screeched. "The pirates won. No one else needs to die." He stood over me, his rifle pointed at Akar's twitching form.

I climbed to my feet.

Qwalm bowed to me and held out his rifle. "I surrender."

The few hunters who remained standing dropped their weapons.

I took the rifle.

Klate limped to Likkil and knelt. "Doc, get over here."

Doc scurried to Likkil. Blood darkened her red shirt. Doc began bandaging the wound. Likkil tried to sit up, but Klate pushed her back down. "I'll be back, cousin." He stood, his gaze focused on Qwalm and me.

Qwalm's feathers trembled. He stayed in his bowed position, his eyes on Klate. Seeing Qwalm terrified unsettled me. I wanted to tell him Klate wasn't going to hurt him, but I stayed quiet.

Tenned strode through the bodies of stunned hunters and pirates. "Get on the floor and put your hands on your head. You're beaten."

Qwalm sank to his belly. Tenned came to him first, probably because he was likely the most dangerous hunter who hadn't been shot. He grabbed Qwalm's own handcuffs and cuffed him. He kicked Qwalm onto his side so he could hobble him.

"He saved my life," I said. "He's not going to do anything."

"He's still a Torf hunter." Tenned grabbed a set of hobbles from a stunned hunter. "I'll need to muzzle him too."

"Tenned," Klate growled.

Tenned paused.

"Leave that Torf alone."

Tenned sighed. "Keep an eye on him."

Qwalm rolled back onto his belly. His terrified gaze still focused on Klate, even though Tenned was the one who disliked him.

Tenned went back to restraining the other hunters with their own cuffs.

Klate growled, loud enough to get the attention of everyone in the room. "We will not harm you hunters. We'll treat your injuries and sell you on Tupra. They'll put you to work, but they don't have pits there."

Qwalm's feathers drooped.

Guilt pulsed through me. No matter what I did, people suffered for it.

Klate pulled out his datsheet and spoke into it. "Amellia, what are the other two ships doing?"

"They're coming toward us. They seem suspicious, but they aren't trying to board," Amellia said.

Klate turned back to the crew. "Get the uninjured hunters to the cages in the hold, and get these ships operational." Klate limped back to Likkil. "Can she be moved?" he asked Doc.

"Yes."

Klate grabbed one of Likkil's arms and lifted her to her feet. He limped toward the infirmary with her while Tenned herded the captured hunters toward the hold. The hunters who remained standing dragged Akar and a few of the other downed hunters.

I itched to look through a window. There were still two more hunter ships out there. Did they know we'd won?

"Krys, can you help me?" Doc asked. He stood over a prone Chix. "This one's got broken bones."

I knelt by the Chix. She had four parallel scratches across her suit, probably from Klate. Those weren't deep, but a leg and arm were bent at odd angles.

I gently scooped the Chix into my arms. She moaned.

"I'll see if I can find the hunters' medic if they have one," Doc said. "You get her to the infirmary."

I carried the Chix to the infirmary. There were more beds than before. I lay the Chix on one of them, one that had a wrinkled look like it had been in storage. Likkil already lay on another bed. The Elba hunter wasn't there. Klate sat by Likkil. He had cleaned the salve off his wound and started gluing the cuts together.

He looked at me. "Are you hurt?"

I took stock of myself. "My face needs some fresh skin. I think I've got a few broken bones in my hand." I held up my swollen and bruised hand. Now that the action was over, it throbbed.

My hand brought me back to how I'd punched Reva in the throat. I tried to hold back tears, but I felt my face wrinkling. She'd been my aunt and I killed her.

"What's wrong?" Klate asked.

"I killed Reva." My real eye blurred with tears. "I hit her in the throat. She had a killing pistol." I shouldn't have hit her in the throat. I should have known that would kill her. "I didn't think."

Klate pressed his wound together and stood. He limped to me and wrapped one of his hairy arms around my shoulders. "It's okay. You did what you had to."

I kept replaying the image in my head. She'd fallen off me so fast, then hit her head. "I should have hit her in the shoulder or her gun hand."

Klate squeezed me tighter. "She didn't give you time to think. Sometimes, there's no other choice."

I sniffed and tried to convince myself Klate was right. It didn't matter what side I took, I always had regrets. She'd been trying to kill me, but if I'd been less panicked, I could've avoided killing her.

CHAPTER FOURTEEN
Pirate

Ralkom quickly patched the hole in the *Deathhorn* before taking over the hunter ship and detaching. By then, the hijacker was disabled, leaving the *Deathhorn* free.

"Come to the cockpit," Klate said.

I followed him to the cockpit. Amellia and Hirami were there. Klate took a chair. I used restraints on the wall to fasten myself in.

We turned to face the enemy. There were two minor bullet fighters and a second major bullet fighter that showed up during the boarding.

"Ralkom, you ready?" Klate asked through the com.

"Yes, Captain," Ralkom said through the speakers. "Let's give them some lasers. Keep your belly out of range. That patch can't take punishment."

"I know," Amellia said.

The bullet fighters opened fire.

We were flying crippled, unable to turn on our shields or go anywhere near lightspeed, but we could still fight. Ralkom would have to do much of the work.

Hirami fired off a volley of lasers as Amellia dove. Hirami fired again, hitting one of the minor bullet fighters. The armored hull melted. At our distance, I couldn't tell if the ship had been breached, but it retreated. We'd frightened it.

The *Deathhorn* vibrated from a laser impact. Above us, the major bullet fighter bore down. One good hit from its laser cannons would destroy us.

Hirami kept shooting.

In the distance, Ralkom fought against the other minor bullet fighter. By the way it weaved and switched direction, it had to be piloted by a Chix. If Ralkom took his focus off it for a second, he'd be shot.

The minor fighter Hirami shot flew at us firing lasers. The lasers were all but invisible against the black vacuum of space, but the gun barrels glowed.

"Hold on!" Amellia flipped a switch.

The *Deathhorn* shuddered. The restraints held me in place. Amellia had hit the reverse thrusters. The major and minor bullet fighters surged past us.

"Hit the minor," Amellia ordered.

Hirami opened up on the smaller fighter. Part of its armor heated up and glowed, but it moved before Hirami could get a killing shot.

The major fighter spun around. Its huge guns swiveled toward us.

A bird-like shadow blocked the stars above us. The major fighter's side melted under a laser blast.

"Good shooting, *Nightslayer*!" Amellia shouted into our com.

"We've got your tail!" A Skallan replied.

My stomach flopped. The *Nightslayer* was Nazar's ship. Had they rescued him?

The *Nightslayer* banked hard and shot after the bullet fighter chasing Ralkom.

"They've got a Chix pilot, don't they?" I asked.

"You don't see normal pilots turn like that," Klate said.

The two remaining minor ships retreated, but the *Nightslayer* zoomed after them and out of sight.

Klate shook himself. "We made it."

"Do we need to help the *Nightslayer*?" I asked. I prayed we wouldn't meet. If Nazar was with the crew, he'd recognize me. If he wasn't, it would mean I got them killed.

"No. They'll manage this without us." Klate squinted at me. "Is something bothering you?"

"I helped capture two of their crew, Nazar and an Elba kid." I rubbed my sore hand.

Klate shrugged. "I heard they did a big attack recently. I'm guessing they got him back, or they'd be stalking Saddat now."

Relief surged through me. Nazar hadn't been confident without reason. "What now?" I gazed at the blackness of space.

"Ralkom will patch the ship up a little better, then we'll head for Tupra. We need to get rid of these hunters." Klate stood and limped from the cockpit.

Ralkom made a better patch for the *Deathhorn* and checked the places that took hits. After he assured Klate his ship could make it to Tupra, we traveled there. Luckily, the ship held together until we headed for the largest moon, which orbited just outside Tupra's asteroid field. We couldn't risk going through the field with weak spots in the hull, and atmosphere entry would be dangerous too.

"Krys, want to watch the landing?" Klate asked from the cockpit.

I hurried to the cockpit. I'd healed from my bullet wound. Now, my hand hurt worse, though the brace Doc gave me helped.

The *Deathhorn* landed on one of the many short landing strips. A few had craters in them, some from asteroids and others from bombings. Amellia drove the *Deathhorn* into a huge door in the mountain. An airshield kept the air from escaping into the moon's vacuum.

Once we were in, the gigantic doors of the spaceport slid closed. A few old ships, some of which were stripped down for parts, sat in a corner. With no atmosphere and lower gravity, landing damaged ships on the moon for repairs made more sense than risking entry into Tupra's turbulent atmosphere.

Amellia began the shutdown procedure.

Klate left the cockpit. I fell in behind him. It was odd how he'd always offer to let me in the cockpit when he had an entire crew. Then again, I was the new person. That was probably why he'd given me special treatment.

The *Deathhorn's* gravity flipped off, leaving us on moon gravity. I smiled. Low gravity was fun, much easier to deal with than zero g.

Klate stopped in the infirmary. Likkil and the Chix hunter were the only ones who hadn't been released by Doc.

Doc's tail twitched. "How's your hand?"

I held my hand out. Doc removed the brace and pulled out his datsheet, which was a medical model. He scanned my hand. "It's healing well. The bones weren't that badly damaged to begin with, and you're young."

"Thanks." I put the brace back on.

Doc's eye and camera turned to Klate. "How about your wounds?"

"They're healing." Klate glanced at the hunter Chix. "What about her?"

Doc's tail twitched. "She'll go to trial. They'll decide what to do with her. No one's buying one that badly injured. We should be able to sell the Elba. I looked and he's got a record here. Turns out he went hunter after he got in trouble with Tupran law."

"Fine with me." Klate left the room.

I bounced after him in the low gravity.

We made it to the hold. Fresh air from the spaceport flowed through the open hatch.

The hunters huddled in two cages. A few were still recovering from their injuries. They were no longer shackled. In the cages, they wouldn't have much choice but to do as they were told.

While Klate walked down the ramp and into the spaceport, I headed toward the cages. Why? I didn't want to see the prisoners, not again. I'd avoided them for the whole week we'd been in space.

"You!" Akar shouted. He slammed into the bars.

At least he was alive.

I stepped closer. The other hunters stayed back. Most likely, they didn't want to be associated with a hunter who ticked off pirates.

"You are a disgrace to Brok and God." Tears ran down his dirty face. "Brok would be ashamed of you."

I flinched. Dad died because of me. So had Reva.

Qwalm, who was in the other cell, stepped toward the bars, his eyes on Akar. "She may be guilty of switching sides, but Reva's death is on her own hands. Her stun pistol was still holstered."

Akar glared at Qwalm. "I should have known a Torf like you would side with pirates."

Qwalm hissed and stomped his foot. "I'm no traitor." His feathers shot up. The hunters imprisoned with him backed away.

"Get out of here!" Akar yelled at me.

I backed away from the only close kin I had left in the galaxy unless Urkot survived. Once I made it out of Akar's sight, I ran out of the ship, the low lunar gravity giving me an extra boost.

I tried to stop at the bottom of the ramp. I tripped and bounced across the hard floor. Pain shot through my hand and leg. I climbed to my feet. At least with the low gravity, I hadn't been badly injured.

I wiped my eye. With the hand brace, it made the operation more difficult than it should have been.

Klate stood under the *Deathhorn*. He gazed up at a hole Ralkom worked to repair properly.

A few other pirate ships, including the *Nightslayer*, were docked in the huge spaceport. I spotted a young red Elba and a Skallan who might have been Nazar.

Klate looked at me. I turned the real side of my face away from him, trying to hide my emotions.

"Do you want something?" Klate asked.

"I want you to let Qwalm go." The words were out of my mouth the second the idea entered my mind.

"The dark Torf?" Klate's ears perked.

"That's him. He saved my life."

"And what about your uncle?" Klate spoke quietly, his voice unreadable.

I stared at the ground.

"Is there any reason, other than family ties, that he should be freed while we sell the others?"

I shook my head. He hated me.

Klate knelt in front of me. "I heard what he said about Brok."

I sniffed. What would Dad think of me now? I'd killed his sister, and I couldn't say anything good in his brother's defense.

"He's wrong," Klate said. "I may not have known your father, but I do know he taught you right from wrong. He might not have realized that teaching would lead you to join pirates, but even so, you did what he taught you."

I wiped more tears from my eye. Akar's words still stung.

"Once we're on Tupra, I'll free Qwalm. I have a feeling you'd break him out if I didn't." Klate said. "I'm not letting Akar go. There's too much chance he'd try to get revenge against you or my crew."

I nodded. No matter what I did, I had guilt eating at me. At least Klate had taken the choice to free Akar away from me. Looking back, I'd only worried about Qwalm's freedom, never Akar's. "Thanks," I said.

"Don't worry about it." Klate stood. "I get no joy out of selling hunters. They'll be slaves, but Trader Town has a lot of laws related to the treatment of slaves. They'll be tried and sentenced, much like in Company space, so some of the ones who had the sense to use stunners might get released after a few years of work."

Tupra hadn't gotten any warmer since my last visit, not a surprise, considering a year there was at least a year and a half on Saddat.

The hunters were cuffed in preparation for the market. Tenned began herding them off the ship.

Akar glared at me, his eyes full of hatred. Klate was right to sell him. If Akar got the chance, he'd kill me.

"Qwalm, wait," Klate said.

Qwalm froze. The other hunters hurried past him like they thought they could be targeted for whatever nefarious plan Klate had in mind.

Tenned squinted at me before herding the rest of the hunters off the ramp and into Tupra's cold mist.

Qwalm flattened his feathers against his body in an attempt to make himself smaller.

Klate approached Qwalm.

Qwalm shifted from foot to foot, like he wanted to run but had nowhere to go.

I hurried to Klate's side.

Klate motioned to me with his head. "Krys asked me to release you." He pulled a key from his belt and reached to unlock Qwalm's cuffs.

Qwalm flinched at Klate's touch. The cuffs fell from his wrists. Qwalm bowed his head to me. "Thank you, Krys."

"You saved my life."

Qwalm motioned toward the ramp. "Walk with me for a ways."

I glanced at Klate.

"What you do is up to you," he said.

I followed Qwalm off the ship. We walked to the edge of the spaceport. He looked around, then stopped. "No matter what you decide, I won't report you."

"Decide what?"

"What you're going to do." Qwalm shifted feet and looked at the ground. "If you want to work with me, we can be a team. We can hunt together like planned. Your family didn't want to tarnish the Karzil name by reporting you, so you're still safe, and I can convince Urkot you're dead."

I pictured hunting with Qwalm. It would be a steady job, and together, we'd be able to avoid taking innocent bounties. Maybe we could even team up with the *Samaritan* and get bounties like Nerrini from Tupra.

"Why were you aboard that ship?" I asked.

Qwalm shifted from foot to foot. "Got paid for being on there, even if we never boarded anyone. Thought it would be easy coin. The Ordained want the pirates gone. You know our rulers are set in place by God."

My optimism evaporated. I couldn't live under the Ordained, or Company, not now. "I can't work for them, not when they've enslaved so many innocent people."

Qwalm's feathers drooped. "I understand." His eyes narrowed. "Are you going to be a pirate?"

I glanced toward the *Deathhorn*. "I don't know."

"I won't judge you if you do but don't compromise, no matter what side you choose. Remember, the Company is stepping up their war against piracy. It's going to get harder."

"Thanks for the advice." My mind churned. "Goodbye."

"Goodbye, Krys," Qwalm said. He strode out of the walled spaceport and into the town. Being a Torf, anyone who saw him would assume he was one of the many Torfs who sided with Tupra.

I headed back toward the *Deathhorn*, my mind still churning through the possibilities of what I should do. With Qwalm's promise to not report me, I could get away with going back to Company space, but what would I do there? I couldn't live my whole life washing tables. Even if I could give up the dream of being a hunter, I still needed to help people.

Before I made it to the ramp, Melsha met me. Her tail swished, fast enough I guessed she was glad to see me. "So, you decided not to go with that hunter?"

I nodded.

"You joining the crew?"

"I don't know." I looked at the ground. "I was a hunter too long to be fighting them."

"Most we do is smuggling," Melsha said. "Getting bendsteel from Lokostwa or Derbis and taking it to Saddat, Chibbink, or even Korska." She smiled. "Our attacks are almost always against slave ships. Free the slaves and sell the owners."

Hirami glided out the *Deathhorn's* hatch and landed a short distance from the ship. He ran through the spaceport and past the guards at the open gates.

A few other kids of various species ran to meet him.

My cybernetic eye magnified the view. One of the Human children had a blue slave tattoo. I watched them run after Hirami, happy and free.

"I'll talk to Klate." I strode up the ramp and into the hold.

Klate stood in the back of the hold counting nigotum cells. His green pants were no longer stained with the blood he'd spilled to save me. I recalled everything he'd done in the time I'd known him. I could trust him to do what was right.

He turned, his ears pricking. "So, the hunter didn't convince you to run away?"

"No." I paused, trying to work up my courage. "Would you like a new crew member? I'm not much of a fighter, but I think you're doing the right thing, raiding slave ships and all."

"I hoped you'd ask." Klate smiled. "It's time this ship had some new blood. Who knows, you might even make captain someday."

I tried to wrap my thoughts around the crazy idea. "I'm not captain material." Tenned would never accept me as captain.

"Don't cut yourself short. Besides, by the time you got to that rank, most of this crew would be retired." Klate patted my shoulder. "There will be plenty of excitement until then. After all, there's no bounty on your head, so you'll be our public face until you've got a bounty."

I smiled. A bounty on my head would be a small price to pay for doing the right thing.

Glossary

SPECIES

Varsillian
(Tupra)

Elba
(Tupra)

Skallan
(Saddat)

Gorkam
(Lokostwa)

Torf
(Lokostwa)

Chix
(Chibbink)

Chix: Chix are arboreal omnivores native to Chibbink. They have gliding skin between their arms and legs and a furry tail that helps them balance in the trees and steer during a glide. While they appear rodent-like, they share no relation to rodents and find being compared to rodents to be an insult.

Though they rarely stand over three feet tall, their military is a force to be reckoned with. Their fast reflexes and spatial awareness make them the best pilots in the Known Region. This gives any Chix-piloted aircraft a distinct advantage. On the ground, they make up for their small size by riding huge predatory warhounds into battle, which is enough to strike terror into their enemies.

Elba: Native to Tupra, Elbas are the biggest species in the Known Region and have a slightly feline-like appearance. Their coat colors vary from black, brown, and red, to blond and white. Those in the Southern Hemisphere tend to have spots, while the northern races have stripes. With large claws meant for tunneling and a powerful upper body, they make dangerous fighters. Though their long-range vision is poor, their night vision and echolocation give them a huge advantage in the darkness of their massive tunnel systems.

Gorkam: With a tough exoskeleton, Gorkam see no need for clothes. Because Lokostwa is so barren, they travel long distances to find food and water. Though they cannot fly, they use their wings to increase the distance they can leap, a big advantage when crossing mountain ranges. Though they have a fierce appearance and their earth-toned shells can function as armor, most are pacifists of the Martyr sect.

Human: Humans are native to Earth, but two colonies left shortly after the Tower of Babel fell. One colony, the common Humans, settled on Chibbink. Common Humans tend to have red or blond hair and green or blue eyes, as well as fair skin. The hisrut race is covered in dark hair. They tend to be shorter and more slenderly built. They have dark eyes and dark skin. Earth Humans inhabit Derbis, but outside a few traders, there is no contact between them and those in the Known Region.

Skallan: Skallan are a semi-coldblooded species native to Saddat. Like the Chix and Humans, they were one of the first space-faring races. They own much of the Company, which puts them in high regard with the Chix and Humans. Their extreme capitalistic culture has led to a massive force of mercenaries and bounty hunters in place of traditional militaries and law enforcement.

They tend to be slender and a little taller than the average Human. From a distance, they could be mistaken for Human, but up close, their green or brown scales, lack of a nose, and their golden, orange, or red eyes leave no doubt that they are far from Human.

Torf: This theropod-like Lokostwan species is known for their endurance and speed. They have sharp teeth so they can strip plants of leaves and bark, but they're also known for eating anything they can catch. They typically have earth-toned feathers, with black and white being extremely rare. Other than during extremely severe weather, Torfs never wear clothing, other than belts that allow them to carry tools or weaponry. They sport a long inner claw on each three-toed foot, giving them a lethal kick, as well as a long feathery tail that helps with balance during fast turns.

Varsillian: This arboreal species lives near the equatorial regions of Tupra. They can change their scale color at will or when they experience strong emotions, making them experts at hiding since they don't wear clothes. They're vegetarians who use their sharp teeth to rip through the outer hulls of fruit to get to the juicy inner flesh. Like Gorkam, they rarely leave their home planet. Some people find them unsettling because of their serpentine bodies and tentacle-like limbs, even though they have little ability in the way of fighting.

Planets

Chibbink: Home of the Chix and common Humans, also known for being the most populated planet in the Known Region. The planet is mostly ocean, and the land is very tropical in nature. It has a large continent in the northern hemisphere and a smaller one in the south, as well as various island chains. Most of the land is swamp and jungle with a few plains on the southern continent. Because their years are only forty days long, the seasons are mild.
Most of Chibbink's fuel reserves are under their ocean, making it hard to mine.

Derbis: A planet so rich in metals that there are more metals on one of the continents than stone. It was recently colonized by Humans, who live exclusively on the steel continent, while the other land masses are inhabited by a sentient flying species.

Lokostwa: A cool planet with only small seas. The planet is arid with no forests. The majority of the planet is grassland or desert with barren mountain ranges. The two sentient species on the planet, Torfs and Gorkam, travel long distances to find enough food to survive. Because of this, Lokostwa is the least populated planet of the four planets in the Known Region.
However, the planet is rich in metal deposits, much more so than Saddat or Chibbink, making it a top exporter of metal. Unfortunately, the Company has taken control of the metals, leaving a huge gap in wealth between the nobility and everyone else. Their years are 368 days long.

Korska: A distant planet past the Known Region. The hisrut Humans live there, as well as other species who are not well-known. The planet has one dark and one light side, making the majority of it uninhabitable. Warlords fight for control of the dusk and dawn regions that are habitable. The planet has no laws, other than the whim of whatever warlord is in control, making it a favorite hiding place for outlaws.

Saddat: The Company, which was the first group to develop economic space travel, originated on Saddat. The planet is mainly fertile plains with some deserts and seas. Skallan are the native species. The years are 359 days long and are the regional standard. Saddat has the most advanced buildings and cities.

Tupra: With years that are 533 days long, Tupra is known for its lethal winters. The planet is extremely mountainous and the land is shrouded in clouds that hide the asteroid-filled sky. Many forests are made of land coral that is perfect for the arboreal Varsillian to inhabit. The mountains are riddled with tunnels, some natural and others dug by Elbas. It has a high concentration of fuel and metals, which would make it a prize for the Company, but the planet's winter and the Elbas are too much for the Company's combination of Chix cavalry and Skallan mercenaries.

About the Author

Jessi lives and works on her family's cattle ranch in eastern Montana. She has some cows, a golden retriever, and a few horses.

Her head is full of wild sci-fi story ideas involving apocalypses, werewolves, and aliens.

Find more, including an illustrated species glossary, on jessilroberts.wordpress.com

Acknowledgments

There are so many people who helped critique and edit this book that I know I've lost track, and if I wrote it down, I'd miss someone or at the very least, misspell someone's name. So a big thank you to all those who helped make this book better, and thank you for your encouragement.

A special thanks to Bryan Davis, who encouraged me to go to my first writers conference and set off my journey to publication.